C

Biggs
is
NOT *Mad*

Lottie Biggs

10A (Top Set)

English Coursework:

Extended Personal Writing

this BOOk Is DeDICateD tO

fl aND NOOse

fOr the haPPY memOrIes Of
seLLING shOes tOGether.

Lottie Biggs is **Not** Mad

by Hayley Long

MACMILLAN CHILDREN'S BOOKS

First published 2009 by Macmillan Children's Books
a division of Macmillan Publishers Limited
20 New Wharf Road, London N1 9RR
Basingstoke and Oxford
Associated companies throughout the world
www.panmacmillan.com

ISBN 978-0-330-47973-8

5 7 9 8 6 4

A CIP catalogue record for this book is available from
the British Library.

Typeset by Nigel Hazle
Printed and bound in the UK by CPI Mackays, Chatham ME5 8TD

iNtrODuCtiONs aND aLL that
YawNY-YawN BOriNG stuff

My name is Lottie Biggs, and in three weeks' time I will be fifteen years old. At school most people call me Lottie Not-Very-Biggs. I've never found this particularly funny. I am five foot and a fraction over half an inch tall. My current hair colour is Melody Deep Plum, which is not as nice as Melody Forest Flame but definitely better than the dodgy custard colour I tried last week. My eyes are bog-standard blue, my chin has a dimple in it and my nose looks like a King Edward potato. My favourite subjects at school are English, history and art, my favourite food is sweet-and-sour chicken and egg-fried rice, and my favourite living person in the whole wide world is my best friend, Goose. My favourite dead person is the actor James Dean. I've got posters of him all over my bedroom walls and on the inside of my bedroom door. I know it's a bit tragic to be erotically attracted to a picture of a dead person, but he does have exceptionally cool hair. When I've finished at school, I'm going to travel round the world, making especially sure that I visit Indonesia so that I can see orang-utans swinging about in the wild. After that, I'm going to settle down with a very rich and handsome film star (one who is NOT dead) and get a job as an art historian in a small gallery somewhere in London like Piccadilly Circus or Trafalgar Square. Until then it looks like I'll have to stick with the occasional snog from Gareth

Stingecombe and my Saturday job, selling shoes in Sole Mates.

This is the kind of yawny-yawn boring stuff that Mr Wood, my English teacher, has asked me to write for my coursework. I have until the end of term to come up with a piece of extended personal writing. That's NEARLY EIGHT WEEKS AWAY. I have no idea how much time Mr Wood expects me to spend writing this thing, but I can tell you right now that I won't be needing nearly eight weeks. A couple of evenings should be ample. Mr Wood says that if I'm ever to achieve the good grade I'm capable of, I need to paint a clear picture of myself in words. He says that I should use the 'blank page as my canvas and the rich vocabulary of the English language as my pallet'.

I asked Mr Wood what *exactly* he meant by this and he said, 'Learn from the Bard,' and gave me a poem to read called 'Sonnet CXXX'. This is a colossally boring title for a poem, I reckon. It was written by the famous expert in creative writing Mr William Shakespeare. Apparently, the Bard was his nickname. The first four lines of 'Sonnet CXXX' go like this:

> 'My Mistres' eyes are nothing like the Sunne,
> Currall is farre more red, than her lips red,
> If snow be white, why then her brests are dun:
> If haires be wiers, black wiers grow on her head:'

When I read this, two things immediately became apparent to me. Firstly, William Shakespeare may have written a lot of stuff that is widely admired, but his spelling was disastrous and, secondly, anybody who looks like this ———▷ has no business being rude about the personal appearance of anybody else. I didn't bother to read the rest of it.

I asked Mr Wood for some further clarification and he said that I need to write something unique and personal in order to give the examiner a flavour of who I am. Now, if I were somebody special like Jennifer Lopez or Christina Aguilera or Beyoncé Knowles this would be a fairly easy task, but it's much harder to be unique and flavoursome when your life is pretty much stuffed solid with school and Sole Mates. I'm so bogged down with coursework assignments and selling shoes that I don't actually have a proper social life. I don't even have a boyfriend. Unless you count Gareth Stingecombe – which I totally DON'T. So, in order to get around the problem of not being a pop star, not having psychic powers, not being the mother of alien triplets and, in short, not being in ANY WAY remotely interesting whatsoever, I'm just going to keep on writing as much about myself as I can. And then, hopefully, when I've finished, there'll be enough reasonable stuff to cobble something together to give to Mr Wood. So here goes . . .

Seeing as how it's practically the only part of my amaZZzing life which is not connected to school, I'll start with Sole Mates. Sole Mates is a shop which sells shoes. You could be forgiven for not knowing this because Sole Mates is not a very helpful name. If I were going to open a shoe shop, I would call it something like New Shooz or the Shupermarket. At least that way, everyone would know what they were going to find inside. I've worked in Sole Mates for four whole months now and half the people I talk to think I work in a fish shop and the other half think it's some kind of dating agency. In fact, it's only the brainy people who actually work out that we're selling shoes and, as the only brainy people in this entire place are me and my best friend Goose, that doesn't leave too many of us who get the joke. And believe me, we're not exactly laughing our heads off.

Mind you, it gets worse. Next door to Sole Mates is a chippy called

and next door to that is a CD and
record shop
called

and go two further along from that
and you come to

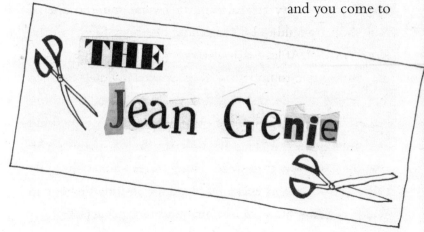

which would be perfectly fine if they sold jeans and stuff, but
they don't. In actual fact, it's a hairdressers' owned by Gareth
Stingecombe's mum. And guess what! Her name is Jean!!!

If you walked any further to the right, you'd be approaching
the flyover and, unless you are the type of freakoid who gets
a weird thrill out of walking on a very narrow pavement one

5

hundred metres up in the air with four lanes of fast-moving traffic whizzing by you, I'd strongly advise against it.

The main street in Whitchurch, where I live, is called Merthyr Road and at the top of it, where the Hippo Eater pub is and just about where the cars come off the flyover, there is a big sign which says:

Croeso i bentref yr Eglwys Newydd
Welcome to Whitchurch Village

Gyrrwch yn ofalus os gwelwch yn dda
Please drive carefully

Obviously this sign welcomes people, in English and in Welsh, to Whitchurch, which is a lovely idea except that:

a) Although Whitchurch is in Wales, I don't know anyone around here who actually speaks Welsh – except Mrs Rowlands (who is evil) and Mr Daniels (who is sweet but leaving our school soon – probably because he's scared of Mrs Rowlands) and they both have to speak Welsh because it's their job to teach it; – and

b) Whitchurch is not a village. Strictly speaking, it's a part
   of Cardiff – just a much less interesting part than the city
   centre.
Anyway, I think that the council should make that sign a bit
bigger and add another line.

Croeso i bentref yr Eglwys Newydd
Welcome to Whitchurch Village

Gyrrwch yn ofalus os gwelwch yn dda
Please drive carefully

Cartref i siopau ag enwau twp
Home to shops with stupid names

Or better still, they should just scrap it altogether and design
a completely new one. Mr Spanton, my art teacher, says I am
a keen visual learner with a naturally artistic streak, so if the
council wanted I'd be perfectly happy to design it for them.
I wouldn't have any Welsh words on my sign because that
would involve me having to enlist the help of Mrs Rowlands

at school and she hates me, which makes communication between us quite stressful. My sign would look something like this:

<u>Beware</u>, You Are Now Entering Whitchurch
which is a great place to buy polo-neck knickers and washing-up bowls but a useless place to buy art materials and non-embarrassing trainers.
Home to Lottie Biggs and Goose McKenzie who both can't wait to get out but need to get their GCSEs first (apparently)
I'd keep driving

A word about Goose. Goose McKenzie is COOL. She is already fifteen. Like me, she lives in appreciation of James Dean, Melody hair products and GCSE art lessons, but unlike me she thinks that history is for dead people and sixth form will be tragic. That's OK, because when Goose leaves school she is going to be a solo folk-rock singer/songwriter and guitarist, and – as she told me herself just the other day – this means her GCSEs are 'essentially superfluous'.

Goose is good with words. I am as well, but Goose is

even better. She always gets top marks in English without even trying, and in her spare time she writes enlightening verse and electrifying song lyrics which are ripped straight from the core of her soul. Goose says that she is planning to secure a six-figure record deal by the time she is eighteen years old. She says that this will allow her to travel far beyond the limiting confines of Whitchurch and bring her into contact with other like-minded Bohemians who are equally cursed and blessed with the burdensome gift of an artistic temperament. Goose especially wants to travel to Iceland, because it is in total darkness for six whole months of the year and she says that this will encourage her to stay indoors and be creative. Goose can be quite deep and intellectual sometimes. She says that she is an Existentialist Absurdist, which means that she thinks her life is ridiculous. Goose says that I'm an Existentialist Absurdist too, but I'm not sure. My mum just says I'm awkward. She even tried to make me see a counsellor once to cure it. Sometimes Goose has 'Existential Days' and on these days I don't see much of her because she tends to stay in her bedroom and think. It doesn't bother her though. Whenever she's in an intense mood she likes to harness her negative energy and turn it into something good by using it as an inspiration for her songwriting. It doesn't bother me either. She's my best friend and I love her.

Life at the sCattY eND Of the street, BaCkwarDs Names aND the YOu PaYs

Sole Mates is at the scatty end of the Merthyr Road. All the places worth hanging out at are up the other end. To be strictly honest, there's not *that* much going on up there either, but there is at least UneeQ Boutique, which sells a good range of urban accessories and fake tattoos, and the Dragon Coffee House, where me and Goose sometimes go for a double choco-mochaccino (with extra cream and marshmallows) and a chat. There's also the public garden, which is really quite blatantly just a big traffic island in the middle of a T-junction. The council has tried to make a feature of it by planting some daffodils and putting a bench or two there so that tired shoppers can rest for a while and admire the passing cars and the premium view of the graveyard. Some do, but mostly the only people who sit there are Elvis Presley[1] who is usually drunk and a random selection of goths from the sixth form. A lot of people call Elvis names or take the piss out of him, but I always say hello and give him a smile when I see him. Smiles are free after all, and I reckon if everyone smiled a bit more there'd be fewer heart attacks and murders and stuff. I also smile and say hello to the sixth-form boys. Most of them are fairly ugly, but it's always worth keeping an eye on them just in case.

---

[1] Not the real one but a fat looky-likey from somewhere up the valley.

And then, just opposite the garden and the last shop before you come to the graveyard, there's Suitably Booted. Now don't get me wrong, Suitably Booted sells shoes which are even more dreadful than Sole Mates. And the name is not good either, by anyone's standards. But it's still a prime location for hanging-out and always will be while Neil Adam works there. To put it quite simply, Neil Adam is LUSH. In fact, I'd go as far as to say that he is SEXADELIC. He has flaxen blond hair which grows right down to his shoulders and razor-sharp cheekbones that would look very good pressed right up next to mine in our wedding photo. I do think his parents have got a lot to answer for though. Bringing a person into this world is a very big deal, I reckon, and giving that person a name is just as big a deal. So WHY ON EARTH his parents have given him a name which spelt backwards is actually MAD ALIEN is absolutely beyond me. A thing like what your name is backwards is very important. Sometimes it can tell you a lot about a person. Take Lee Fogel, for instance. He's in my double-science class and it occurred to me one day while Mr Thomas was droning on and on about electrical circuits and ticker-tape timers and other random pointless stuff that Lee Fogel's name is actually LEG OF EEL backwards. As far as I know, there is nothing wrong with Lee's leg, but I do think that he's a pretty slippery character. My name backwards is either SGGIB ETTOLRAHC or SGIBB EITTOL, depending on whether or not you are my friend, and while I agree that neither way is very pretty or easy to pronounce, at least it doesn't reveal anything sly about me. Having said all that, the fact that Neil Adam is a mad alien when viewed from a different angle still would not stop me from going out with him if he asked.

Goose fancies Neil Adam as well. She once tried to express her emotions on this subject by writing a song about him. It was called 'Song for Neil', and with her permission I have a reproduction of the lyrics right here.

Song for Neil
By Goose McKenzie

My heartbreakingly handsome Neil
You wear cool clothes and have hunk appeal
When you look my way I want to squeal
And squawk and hop like a cockatiel
My heart, it starts to cartwheel
Upside down and head over heel
And for a nano-second I almost reveal
That my love for you is not plastic but real
But maddeningly still you conceal
The desire which you obviously feel
I'm begging you now please end my ordeal
Because frankly Neil
You're behaving like an imbecile.
So take me out for a meal
That would be flipping ideal
We could eat chips and veal
Followed by a snog and a quick feel.

Personally I don't think that Goose got anywhere close to conveying the pure physical beauty of Neil Adam, and I don't think that Goose was that chuffed with her effort either because she never bothered to develop it into a proper song. She says that as songwriting goes, it's a bit basic. She says she might use it as a filler track on her album though.

Neil Adam is the Saturday sales assistant at Suitably Booted, and as he goes to a private school in Cardiff city centre this is the only contact we ever have with him. As contact goes, it falls well below the satisfactory standard. Sometimes one or other of us will visit his shop on our lunch break and pretend to be interested in buying a pair of old ladies' indoor slippers or peep-toe sandals in the hope that he will serve us, and sometimes, if we're really lucky, Dionne, our manageress at Sole Mates, will send us up to Neil's shop to borrow his hoover or something. So he does know that we exist. It's just that he doesn't seem very excited about that fact yet.

I'm Head Saturday Girl at Sole Mates. I'm not actually sure that I should be empowered with such a position of responsibility because I'm still not quite fifteen, but, to be honest, I don't think that Dionne, my manageress, is all that bothered about the finer details of employment law. Thanks to me, Goose works in Sole Mates too. She started two weeks after I did. All I had to do was put in a good word and Dionne rang her up the same day. Goose arrived for an interview within the hour wearing the most grotesque skirt that I've ever seen in my life. I think she must have borrowed it from her mum. When Dionne asked her why she wanted the job, Goose went tomato red and whispered, 'I truly believe I can help you sell more shoes, and also it would get me out of the house and stop me spending all my time doing homework.'

She was very convincing. If she hadn't been around my house until eleven o'clock the night before watching *Free Willy 2*, I might even have believed her myself.

Dionne smiled and looked at Goose as if she wanted to eat her all up. And then she gave her a job.

Anyway, just a few weeks later, the last Head Saturday Girl – Scary Mary, who has a metal spike coming out of her face – left to start her college course, leaving ME as the longest-serving member of the Saturday staff. Me and Goose were then joined by Emily, who goes to a girls' school a bit further down the road. Emily is generally quite nice but a little bit lacking in life experience. I think she is frightened of boys. Dionne must think that Emily's a little bit wet too, because even though Emily is the oldest, Dionne said that unless Gina is in, I'm in charge. And as Gina mostly only works during the week and Dionne is nearly always asleep in her office or else looking at Facebook on the Sole Mates computer, this means I *officially* have the power. I think this gets on Goose's nerves a bit, but she does have to remember that I have two weeks' more experience of selling shoes than she does.

As manageresses go, Dionne is OK. I'd even go as far as

to say she is actually fairly cool. She is only twenty-two years old – which is still fairly young, I reckon – dyes her hair Melody Platinum Sun-Kissed – I've seen the boxes in her shopping bags – and doesn't really seem all that interested in shoes. Every Friday night she dollies herself up and shifts her feet to the beat at Gigi's Dance Emporium in town, which means that she spends almost every Saturday asleep in her office with the door locked. This is good.

Gina, on the other hand, is not OK. Gina is deeply annoying. She is getting on a bit – I'd say at least forty – has one of those very loud *luverrly-jubbly* style voices which comes from London and URGENTLY needs an introduction to the world of Melody's hair-colour enhancers. I think it's fair to say that in the battle against grey, Gina's hair has well and truly rolled over and died without a decent fight. To highlight her hair problem further, she persists in wearing it all tied up in one huge side ponytail. The weight of her ponytail together with the weight of the enormous amount of gold she wears means that Gina is almost always leaning to one side. This is not generally a problem for her, but it can make trips up and down the stepladder look particularly treacherous. Gina mostly only works during the week but sometimes, just to throw us out of our comfort zones, she'll rock up on a Saturday and start barking orders. This is blatantly very bad.

Gina is particularly obsessed with the YOU PAYS. She probably dreams about them in her sleep. The YOU PAYS are the round stickers which we have to put inside the most

tragic shoes in order
to get rid of them a
bit quicker.
They look
like this.

ORIGINAL PRICE
£34.99
— YOU PAY —
£6.00

As far as I can tell, the original price is always a figure dreamt up in the vivid imaginations of either Dionne or Gina. Anyway, Gina is OBSESSED with these stickers. I wouldn't even be at all surprised if she has hundreds of these stickers sneakily stuck all over her underwear to give her a warm glow throughout the day. A typical conversation with Gina goes something like this.

Me: Hi, Gina. You in today? You're not usually in on a Saturday.

Gina: Yeah, well, someone's gotta keep an eye on you girls, innit. 'Ave you 'oovered this morning? I can see clumps of dust under that shelf.

Me: I've put Emily in charge of hoovering. Shall I have a word with her?

Gina: Yeah . . . No . . . Yeah . . . Hang about . . . Why are all these YOU PAYS still on the cash desk? In't you sorted these out yet? If you don't put the YOU PAYS out first thing in the morning like I'm always tellin' yah, it's the customer who loses out. 'Ow many times 'ave I got to drum it into you, Missy Biggs? BEGIN NEW DAYS BY DOING THE YOU PAYS.'

Gina's scatty command of grammar really winds me up. Mr Wood, my English teacher, is always telling us that 'there's no such thing as *must of, should of, could of,* it's must *have,* should *have,* could *have*'. Mr Wood says stuff like, 'The day you all get that simple little fact into your tiny little heads is the day I can retire a happy man.' Well, this is all very well and good, but he doesn't need to be moaning on to me about it. Even though I'm Welsh, my English is banging.[2] It's the likes of Gina that he needs to start talking to. Mind you, I'd like to see him try. I reckon Gina could beat Mr Wood to a pulp if she wanted to.

Gina's moan about the YOU PAYS generally lasts for a mean average of seven minutes and twenty-six seconds, but she did once manage an impressive eleven minutes and eighteen seconds. It's only me who is ever on the receiving end of this particular form of moan. Never Goose. Never Emily. Only ME. Sometimes the responsibility of being Head Saturday Girl can be an extremely troublesome and tedious experience.

---

[2] Banging means great. Not to be confused with hanging, which means minging.

hOw Me aND GOOse BeCame frieNDs aND MY LiBeratiNG DisCOverY Of the wOrLD Of artifiCiaL hair COLOraNt

Today in school I showed some of the autobiographical stuff that I have written so far to Mr Wood in order to get an idea of how I am progressing and to see whether I'm heading for a reasonable grade or a fudge grade.[3] Mr Wood looked at my work for about half a millisecond, snorted a bit at something that he blatantly found amusing and then said, 'It's a good start, Charlotte, but rather than rambling on in an unstructured way, you need to concentrate more on one particular episode.'

Mr Wood and I are not close personal friends, which is why he calls me Charlotte. Mind you, he wouldn't call me Lottie even if we *were* friends because Mr Wood doesn't like abbrevies.

I said, 'What kind of particular episode?'

Mr Wood said, 'Something which has had an important effect on your life. A pivotal moment, perhaps. A watershed after which nothing has ever been quite the same again.'

I have to be honest. I've had conversations with Mrs Rowlands the Welsh teacher which have made more sense

---

[3] A *fudge* grade is basically what Gareth Stingecombe is going to see when he opens his exam results. He'll have an F, a U, maybe a D and so on. *Fudge* grades are not good.

– and she hates me. After school, I tried asking Goose if she understood what Mr Wood was on about. We were sitting in my kitchen and we were both feeling a bit the worse for wear because we'd just had a race to see who could eat an entire family bag of marshmallows the fastest. Goose had won. She always does. When I'd finally managed to stop feeling sick I said, 'Woody wants us to base our coursework on a watershed. Do you get it?'

With her little finger Goose hooked a piece of marshmallow out from the inside of her upper lip, wiped her mouth on a tissue and then said, 'I'm not being funny, Lotts, but I tend to find any conversation on the topic of coursework really discombobulating. Do you know what I mean?'

I didn't but I nodded my head anyway and then Goose started telling me about her band, *Goose McKenzie and the Tribe of Pixies*, and I just sort of let the subject drop. When Goose went home, I looked up the word *discombobulate*. It said:

> **dĭscombŏbūlāte** (*verb*) disturb, disconcert.

Goose is one of those people who are pretty AND clever. I still like her though. After that, I looked up the word *watershed* and it said:

> **wa'tershĕd** (*noun*) *1. a line of high land from which streams flow down on each side; 2. a turning point in the course of events.*

I really don't see what high lands and streams have got to do with anything. Whitchurch is fairly flat. If you want to go anywhere near any high land and streams, you need to go up the road to Taff's Well or Caerphilly; they've got hills but they haven't got much of anything else. I don't think they even stretch to streams. Which means that Mr Wood must have been talking about turning points. So why couldn't he have just said that rather than banging on about watersheds and pivots?

Anyway, I have decided that I am going to write about two very important things which have happened to me in my life so far and made a definite impact upon it. The first important thing was becoming best friends with Goose. The second important thing was my introduction to the world of artificial hair colorant. Both these key events are closely related.

Before I became friends with Goose, my hair was brown. I'm not talking sexy brunette; I'm talking more of a mongrel-dog-colour or what my Nan would describe as beige. Yes. Before I was friends with Goose I had BEIGE hair. How I survived with beige hair for fourteen and a half years is a mystery to me, but it probably explains why I am not smiling in any of my school photos.

And then, one day not long after I'd started Year 10, I got moved up into the same English class as Goose. I don't know why. It's not as if I'd grown a new brain or anything. Probably it was just an excuse to get me out of the same group as Samantha Morgan. Me and Samantha Morgan used to be friends in Year 9 but then we stopped being friends and now her mum likes her to keep away from me. Anyway, I'd gone along to my usual English class and my teacher had told me I was being moved up into the top set. Everyone else in the group looked a bit fed up when they heard this, and Gareth Stingecombe called me Brainbox Biggsy which is hardly very original or mature but the best that he could manage without having had several years to think about it beforehand. Even so, I didn't want to appear too blatantly chuffed with myself so I huffed and puffed a bit and said, 'Oh, do I have to?' a couple of times and then left the classroom fairly dramatically without picking my feet up properly.

When I got to Mr Wood's class, I was told to sit down next to Goose as she was the only person who had a space next to her. I don't mind admitting that this was a little bit scary because even though Goose is really pretty, she can look a bit stroppy sometimes. I'd seen her around in the corridor and in the school yard but I didn't know her name or anything and I'd certainly never bothered to speak to her. She only started at my school at the beginning of Year 10 and I don't tend to talk to new people much unless I'm forced to by a form tutor or something. On this occasion, Goose was wearing a padlock round her neck and had purple hair and industrial strength mascara and when Mr Wood said she needed to move her things up to give me some room, she made a hissy noise. When I sat down she whispered, 'Let's just get something clear. I don't mind you sitting there so long as you respect one rule.'

'What's that?' I whispered back.

'Never *ever* refer to me by any name other than Goose.'

'*Goose?*'

Goose looked me straight in the eye and nodded firmly. 'Goose. I don't respond to ANYTHING ELSE. Even the teachers call me Goose.'

'OK,' I said with a shrug. 'Whatever.'

At just that moment Mr Wood stopped writing on the board and turned around and said, 'Charlotte Biggs. Gail McKenzie. Can you both desist from chatting, please?' And then he turned his back on us again and continued writing about apostrophes.

'*Gail?*' I said in a massively loud whisper, and then I clapped my hand over my mouth to stop myself from laughing my head off.

Next to me, Gail McKenzie's face turned totally mega-peeved purple. 'It's a stupid name because I was born during a stupid storm,' she whispered. 'How unlucky is that? Any other day of the year and I'd have been called Zoe.' And she sat back in her chair and looked genuinely discombobulated and I decided, right there and then, that it would be best for everyone if I just respected Goose's wishes on this blatantly sensitive matter. Even if Mr Wood didn't. And anyway, to be fair, she does look much more of a Goose than a Gail.

There was still one thing I wanted to know though. 'Why *Goose?*' I whispered.

Goose sort of smiled. 'I've got really weird feet,' she whispered. 'My dad reckons they're webbed and I must be descended from a duck or something. One day he called me Goose and it kind of stuck.' For the first time ever, Goose gave me a proper big massive smile and said, 'I don't mind – it's heaps better than Gail.'

From the front of the class Mr Wood said loudly, 'WILL YOU TWO BE QUIET?'

I'd completely forgotten about him. I said, 'Sorry, Mr Wood, but we were talking about apostrophes.'

Goose added, 'Yeah, they're actually *really* interesting, aren't they?'

Mr Wood rolled his eyes and muttered something I couldn't quite catch but it didn't sound good. So I put my head down and started copying out all the apostrophe stuff on the board.

I'd written about two words when Goose nudged me and slid a piece of paper over to my side of the desk.

Not being funny but do u know u've got beige hair?

And that was a real pivotal watershed moment in my life because up until that very second it had not even occurred to me that I had the most boring hair colour in the world. I must have looked traumatized because Goose whispered, 'It's all right. I can sort that out for you if you like.'

She did as well. Not right away in the middle of that English lesson obviously. But once we'd got to know each other a bit better and became proper friends and everything, she invited me round her house and dyed my hair for me in her bathroom. Nothing too drastic that first time. Burst Conker. Which was a nice shiny brown colour and MUCH better than beige. When my mum saw it she said that it made me look like Dilwyn, our next-door neighbours' red setter. I got a bit upset then and said, 'Are you saying that I look like a dog?' My mum put her head on one side as if she was thinking extremely hard and said, 'Possibly. But Dilwyn is a very attractive dog, isn't he?'

My mum gets on my nerves sometimes.

Even so, I bet she liked it really. She was probably secretly relieved that she no longer had to live with the shame of having a daughter who has beige hair. Mind you, I reckon my mum is quite open-minded about things like hair dye anyway because she sees and hears a lot of things during the course of her working week. She works at Cardiff Police Station. She doesn't go out chasing criminals any more because she's too old and slow for that now, but she still gets to read about all the muggings and stuff on her computer screen. I reckon it would take a lot more than Burst Conker hair to shock my mum.

Be warned though, hair colorant is not without its hazards. Sometimes things go wrong. Take last Saturday for instance. When I got into work Gina was waiting for me. She didn't bother with a hello or anything polite and normal like that. She just said, 'You're late, Charlotte.'

I looked at my watch and said, 'No, I'm not. It's exactly nine o'clock. I'm bang on time.'

Gina said, 'To be early is to be on time. To be on time is to be late. And to be late is unacceptable.'

She must get these phrases out of a staff handbook.

I didn't want to wind her up any more so I moved out of her way and made a start on labelling the YOU PAYS. Gina is not really the sort of person you should aggravate. By her own admission, she has 'never known the meaning of true love'. This makes her much more touchy than the average person. To be honest, she'd probably have a bit more luck in the love department if she ditched that side ponytail and some of the bling. I didn't tell her this though. I just got on with the YOU PAYS. I'd barely been working for more than two minutes when she interrupted me again and said, 'Aren't you going to ask me where Goose is?'

I was rather surprised by this. Goose is usually a fairly punctual sort of person so I'd assumed she was already in. I put down my YOU PAYS and said, 'Isn't she out the back?'

Gina put her head even further on one side and looked at me with a smile which I can only describe as trying to be omniscient.[4] I say *trying to be* omniscient because it is impossible to look clever when your only interests are YOU PAY stickers. But at least it meant that she had forgotten to be in a bad mood with me. That woman has the memory of

---

[4] This word ranks alongside *blatant*, *haberdashery* and *orang-utan* as an all-time personal favourite. It means 'knowing everything'. For example, *It's pointless trying to convince my mum that I have been working really hard in maths and science because she is omniscient.* By the way, my least favourite words are *gusset*, *armpit* and *grounded*.

a goldfish who has had its brain removed. Gina put her face too close up next to mine and said, 'Ask me where she is.'

Sometimes, with some people, it's best just to play along. I said, 'OK, Gina. Where is Goose?'

'She 'ad to go 'ome.'

Now this really did surprise me. Gina might have all the brain capacity of a particularly thick goldfish, but actually, if the truth be told, it was me who did the best impression of one right then. I looked at her all confused with my mouth open for a second or two and then said, 'What? You mean she's been in and out again already. It's only –' I checked my watch – 'six minutes past nine.'

Gina's eyes twinkled so that they matched her gold jewellery and she started stroking her ponytail as if it was a small fluffy animal. I could tell that she was really enjoying herself. 'Ask me why she 'ad to go 'ome already?'

This was getting more and more pointlessly random. I said, 'OK, Gina. Why has Goose gone home already?'

Gina said, 'I'll tell you why she went 'ome. Her hair was khaki!'

'*What?*'

'I'm telling you, Lottie. She came in. Looking fairly normal. Well, as normal as you two girls ever look. But when I put the strip lighting on, it reflected off her 'air and – I'm telling you – she had khaki-coloured hair. Almost green! Dionne had to send her 'ome to sort it out. We couldn't 'ave 'er in 'ere looking like that. She would 'ave frightened off the customers. She looked like a Brussels sprout!'

She and Emily started laughing then, which annoyed me because I guessed that Goose was going through a very traumatic and upsetting experience. I tried to ignore them, but when I couldn't bear it any longer I left the YOU PAYS and went out the back to sit and think. The stockroom is a very good place for sitting and thinking. Even when we are really busy, it's possible to sit and meditate for quite some time if you know what you're doing. The trick is to climb up the highest stepladder and sit on the platform at the very top. Often it takes Gina ages to realize where you are and then, when she does see you, she thinks that you are getting shoes down for a customer.

I sat and contemplated the colour of Goose's hair for seventeen minutes. I've never seen anyone with khaki hair before and I couldn't quite imagine it. Then my phone beeped. I pulled it out of my pocket. Goose had written:

> **GOOSE**
>
> DONT TRY WALNUT WHIP ON TOP OF SUNKIST PLATINUM!!! NEIL ADAM SAW ME WIV GREEN HAIR. OMG!!!!! BAK SOON GX
>
> OPTIONS   BACK

I had to bite my lip to stop myself from laughing and revealing my hiding place. Even though Goose is my very best friend, the idea of Neil Adam witnessing her at a moment of heightened hair-dye disaster was strangely satisfying. Goose can be far too pretty. Everyone fancies her because she has naturally good bone structure. I, on the other hand, have the bone structure of a Cornish pasty.

I was just about to dial her number so that I could get all the horrible details when I was interrupted by a familiar, irritating voice.

'What you doing up there, Missy Biggs?'

I looked down. Gina was looking right back up at me. 'Oh, I'm trying to find SHANE in size ten in fawn,' I lied.

Gina wrinkled up her brow suspiciously. 'Oo for? There's no one in the shop.'

I gave a big noisy sigh. 'Oh, he must have left. Nice of him to let me know he doesn't want them any more.'

Gina's eyes went all narrow and she looked at me a bit dubiously. 'Yeah, well. SHANE should be there just next to the NIGEL slip-ons, innit. Don't be up there all day.' She stared at me for a few seconds more with her scary eyes and then turned and wandered off. Breathing a sigh of relief, I busied myself with my pretend search for SHANE and pulled a box off the shelf just by where I was sitting. Opening the lid, I took out the shoes which were inside and examined them. They were a nasty cream colour with dark brown stitching down the outer edges. My grandad would have described them as loafers, but I doubt if even he would have worn them. Goose would have described them as putrid. I looked at the label attached to the front of the box and then made an adjustment to it with my pen.

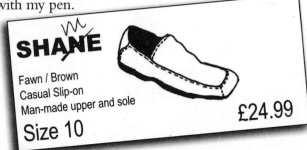

SHANE

Fawn / Brown
Casual Slip-on
Man-made upper and sole

£24.99

Size 10

Placing the box back on the shelf, I couldn't help smiling. No lover of mine would ever be seen dead in a pair of man-made fawn and brown SHANE shoes. Neil Adam, for example, is most definitely not a SHANE type of man. Come to think of it, he's not a khaki-hair-colour type of man either.

Life isN't aLL fuNNY ha ha, aPPareNtLY

Keith Bright has a heavy beard and wears aviator-style tinted reading glasses. Gina thinks that Keith Bright looks like a young Kirk Douglas. I wouldn't know whether this is true or not because I have never actually bothered to establish who Kirk Douglas is, let alone what a young version of him might or might not look like. What *is* clear is that Gina fancies the pants off Keith Bright. And maybe, *just maybe*, she actually has a good chance of him fancying her back because Keith Bright is the owner of Bright Eyes Optician. Which must mean that his vision can't be up to very much.

On the other hand, I'm not sure if Gina *does* have any chance with Keith Bright because I am saddened to say that Keith Bright is secretly in love with me and Goose. This is blatantly very weird and slightly pervy but it is also the truth. Sometimes he stands in his shop window, directly opposite ours, with his arms folded and an expression of desperate desire all over his furry face. Just staring. This sends me and Goose into screaming panicked hysterics but it does make the time pass a little faster. Working in the kind of shoe shop which hardly ever gets any customers can be terrifically boring.

Last Saturday afternoon me and Goose were in the shop and for over forty minutes no one had come in to even so much as browse. Goose had hurried back to work after a super-quick application of Melody Midnight Brown, and although it had definitely taken the edge off the Brussels sprout colour, there was still more than a hint of green when she stood under a light. Considering that Dionne had sent her home at ten to nine and Goose had got back again by twenty past eleven, she had done a fairly reasonable job but it wasn't up to her usual high standard of hair-colour application. One of Goose's ear lobes was a bit brown on the end and she'd dyed most of her scalp as well. I didn't tell her this though in case it turned her existential.

For a while we sorted out the YOU PAYS, and then we re-laced a few pairs of trainers, and then when we'd got bored of that we made Emily do some hoovering, and then, when we'd got bored of *that*, I even did a bit of hoovering myself. By the time I'd finished, Goose had recovered from her hair-dye trauma and was feeling more chatty and we talked about Neil Adam and school and stuff. Goose said that Neil Adam had almost collided straight into her when she had run down the high street that morning with her green hair. Goose said she would have rather been seen by anybody in the entire world at that moment than by him. I said, 'Don't worry, Goose, he probably thought you looked really cool. I mean, how many other people are there around Whitchurch village with green hair?'

This definitely cheered Goose up. Goose is not as easy-going as I am by a long stretch. Apart from the occasional bout of random behaviour and that time last year that I got a three-day exclusion from school for trying to throw Samantha Morgan's desk out of the window, I am *very* easy-going. To cheer Goose up some more, I said, 'Do you want to see the gymnastics routine that I'm preparing for my PE practical?'

Between you and me, I'm not really all that interested in PE but I decided to take it as a GCSE option because the only other choices were RE, French and Welsh. And as Mrs Rowlands the Welsh teacher quite blatantly hates me and as I have precisely no desire at all to be a French vicar, I chose PE.

Goose said, 'OK then − if it'll provide temporary relief from my terminal boredom,' and then helped me to move a rack of tights and a couple of the YOU PAY baskets so that I had a good clear performance area and wouldn't bang my head while executing any of the more complicated gymnastics manoeuvres. I have to admit that I was quite excited by the prospect of performing my routine on the shop floor with a proper audience. The shop floor is a lot bigger than my bedroom floor, and the only audience I ever have at home are my cuddly orang-utan collection and my James Dean posters. And as Gina had gone home a couple of hours earlier with a headache (probably caused by the weight of her side-on ponytail) and as Dionne hadn't surfaced from her office all day, it seemed like a really premium opportunity to get some practice in.

I limbered up my muscles and was all ready to start when Emily said, 'Won't you need some music?'

This was a very good point. Especially from someone who never speaks to boys. It is a well-known scientific fact that all teenagers perform much better in every subject if they are allowed to listen to music while they are working. Me and Goose looked at each other. 'It's your decision, Lottie,' said Goose. 'It'll have to be either Justin Timberhead, Mad Donna or Kylie Binogue.'

Now, if you're thinking that this particular selection of musical artistes sounds putrid in the extreme, you are correct. In our shop, there is a really random rule which stops us from playing any original music to the customers. Instead we get sent specially recorded CDs from head office which contain popular chart songs sung by people we've never heard of whose voices aren't quite good enough. So all day it feels like we're *nearly* listening to proper music but not quite. This is a very aggravating sensation.

After some deliberation, I opted for Mad Donna's attempt at 'Vogue', and Goose and Emily took out a couple of cardboard signs from off the display stands so that they could use the backs to give me a score out of ten. The tension on the shop floor was electric. I took a few deep breaths and threw myself into my routine.

Considering that I don't actually like PE, I have to say that I was really rather good. In only two minutes, I managed several perfect forward rolls, an almost vertical headstand and a reasonably tidy cartwheel. Even Emily was impressed and she never speaks to any boys. Midway through mentally preparing myself to perform the whole thing a second time, Goose's voice interrupted me and broke my thread of concentration.

'Lottie, you've got an audience! Keith Bright is watching.'

I looked up. Keith Bright was standing in the window across the road with his arms folded, just staring at us.

Now Keith Bright might well be a dodgy old optician who is blatantly in love with me and Goose, but he is still a more appreciative audience for my GCSE PE gymnastics routine than my cuddly orang-utans and posters of James Dean. So I cartwheeled over to the window and did a majestic handstand right up against the glass. (Do not fear – I was wearing trousers.) Keith stood looking at us for a few seconds longer and then he turned around and walked away into the back of his optician's.

We knew he'd still be watching though. So we got Emily to turn the music up and me and Goose joined hands to waltz around the shop floor to 'Like a Prayer'. Unfortunately, Goose trod on a TOPSY jelly shoe in pink, which had fallen out of one of the YOU PAY baskets, and she went crashing into the stand of ETHEL indoor slippers next to the till and caused us both to fall on the floor on top of a heap of foam-filled gorilla feet. My leg went a bit dead at this point but I wasn't really thinking about it too much because, all of a sudden, I couldn't stop laughing. Goose was laughing too. We were both laughing so much that neither of us could stand up. I was even finding it quite difficult to breathe because I was laughing so much that my heart hurt. This happens quite a lot actually.

From somewhere out the back, we heard a door slam.

Emily, who never speaks to boys, hurried over to the furthest corner of the shop and started sticking YOU PAYS into the vast quantities of OLGA gym shoes in PVC. Me and Goose remained where we were, on the floor, covered in foam-filled gorilla feet. We were in a laughter-induced state of total uselessness.

'What on earth is going on?'

I looked up and so did Goose. A few helpless giggles hiccupped out of us. Dionne was frowning down, all sun-kissed hair and thunder-filled expression.

'Have you two been mucking about again?'

With some difficulty I stood up. So did Goose. I couldn't speak because my breathing had gone all funny and so had my head, but Goose said, 'It's my fault. I was wiping down the fixtures and fittings to keep myself busy and to keep the shop looking tidy but then a bit of dust got up my nose and made me sneeze really violently, causing me to momentarily lose control of my faculties, and my left arm swung out and thumped Lottie in the face causing her to collide with me and causing the two of us to collide, quite violently actually, with the display of novelty indoor slippers.'

As I mentioned before, Goose is very good with words.

Dionne sucked in her cheeks and made her eyes go so narrow that they almost completely disappeared. 'Really?' she said. 'It's just that Mr Bright across the road says that you've been doing handstands, headstands, roly-polies and the tango!'

Neither of us was expecting this response. I went all red

and started to laugh again, and Goose's mouth fell open. We both turned and looked out across the street. Keith Bright was back, standing in the centre of his display of contact-lens cleaners and spectacle frames. He was holding a mobile phone and smiling. When he saw us looking over at him, he waved. I don't know why but seeing him standing there made me start to laugh AGAIN so hard that I thought my lungs were going to pop.

Through my hysterics I heard Goose say, 'We weren't tango-ing, Dionne. I solemnly swear that there have been no tango activities taking place in this shop.'

Dionne raised an eyebrow. 'Really?'

Goose said, 'Really,' and then, apologetically, she added, 'It was more the waltz, I think.'

Dionne gave a blatantly exasperated sigh and looked at me and Goose for a long time without speaking. Mostly she was looking at me. It weirded me out a bit, and I stopped laughing and started to feel bad. Dionne is all right, to be honest. She is not someone who I deliberately would want to make angry. Not like Mrs Rowlands, my Welsh teacher, for example. I chewed my nail and started looking at the pattern on the carpet. It was of lots and lots of tiny feet shapes arranged in circular spirals. It started to make me feel a bit dizzy. Dionne pointed her finger at each of us and said, 'I don't want any more of it. No more messing around. You understand?'

We both nodded.

Dionne looked at us and frowned. 'And you need to start

acting more responsibly. Life isn't all funny ha ha, you know.' And then she sighed again, waved at Keith and turned to disappear back to her office. As she crossed the shop I caught sight of her reflection in one of the long mirrors. She was smiling to herself, but something about her smile made me go a bit quiet; it was like one of those smiles you see painted on the faces of sad circus clowns. It must just have been the effect of the dodgy fluorescent lighting in our shop.

the Great tiGhts ChaLLeNGe aND resCuiNG esmereLDa

Half an hour before closing time, Dionne called me, Goose and Emily into her office. For a sickly second I felt my belly do a backflip. The only other times I have ever been called into Dionne's office are once when she interviewed me for the job and twice to get my ear bashed over random work-related stuff. I really don't like ear-bashings. I am naturally a very non-confrontational person. Confrontation makes my heart heave and my brain crash and I try to avoid it whenever I can.[5] It also makes me go a bit sweaty and panicky and I was just starting to get the first signs of clammy-skin-syndrome when I remembered that Dionne also wanted to see Emily too, and Emily, as far as I am aware, has never done anything in the remotest bit wrong in her entire life. Not ever. She is the embodiment of everything that is sensible and good. She is Mother Teresa, Lady Diana and Florence Nightingale all rolled into one. And she doesn't talk to boys. Now I'm not saying that Goose and I are horrible, terrible people. We're not. But we *are* normal, and normal people make mistakes once in a while. Like the time Goose got sent home from school for deliberately connecting her Bunsen burner to

---

[5] Orang-utans are also non-confrontational animals. This is one of the reasons why I like them so much. Another reason is that they have the most wickedest shade of ginger hair I have ever encountered anywhere.

the water tap. Or the time I scratched my own name on to the living-room door with a compass. Or the time I put my baby brother's water wings on my ankles and had to be rescued by a lifeguard because I got flipped straight under and swallowed half the swimming pool. I'd be willing to bet my life that Emily has never made a single mistake *ever*. So it was a bit of a comfort to have Emily alongside us just then because it meant that we couldn't possibly be in trouble for once.

'Shut the door behind you, girls, and sit down.' Dionne had kicked her shoes off and was eating a very large custard slice from a paper bag. I noticed that there were quite a few other identical paper bags in the bin by her chair.

'The reason I've called you in is because we need to increase sales figures. I think perhaps we could all pull our weight a little more, don't you?'

Dionne was looking
straight at me, but
I wasn't sure if this
question was
meant for me alone
or all three of us so
I just shrugged
my shoulders
and pulled my
I'm hearing you
face, like this:

Dionne poured herself a coffee and took another mouthful of custard slice.

'I need you girls to be giving it your all one hundred per cent of the time because I'm tied up out the back here doing the paperwork. I can't be keeping an eye on you every minute of the day because I'm just too busy. So what I . . .'

There was a white phone on her desk and it began to buzz like a grasshopper, interrupting her in mid-flow. She picked it up and said in a posh voice, 'Hello, Sole Mates.' Then in a much less posh voice, she said, 'Oh, hi, Suze . . . Yeah . . . No . . . You're kidding me, yeah? . . . Look, I'm working at the mo' but I'll call you back on my mobile in five . . . OK? Bye.'

Dionne replaced the receiver, dropped her custard-slice bag into the bin and continued. 'So what I was thinking was that we all need a little incentive. Start selling things that we haven't been pushing. The shoes sell themselves but I want *you* to start using your sales skills to push other products. And I want to start with the tights. Whoever can sell the most pairs of tights next week wins a prize.'

'What is it?' said Goose.

Dionne smiled. 'Sell the most tights next Saturday and you'll find out.' With one hand, she pulled a very buff flip-top, Bluetooth, MP3 camera phone from her pocket and began to text, and with the other hand she shooed us out of the office. The tights-selling team talk was blatantly over.

Me and Goose left Emily hoovering up out the front and disappeared into the darkest recess of the stockroom for a chat. We took up position at the twin summits of a pair of stepladders.

'Do you think this prize will be worth having?' I asked.

'Who knows?' said Goose, and then added with a shrug, 'Who cares?'

'Maybe it'll be a free pair of shoes,' I said.

Goose snorted. 'Probably. But who'd want them? All the shoes in this shop are putrid. I mean, look at these.'

She pulled a box free from the shelf, but the boxes were packed in so tightly that in releasing one she sent another four boxes crashing to the ground several feet below where we were sitting.

A distant yell from Dionne's office told us to be more careful. Goose rolled her eyes and turned her attention back to the shoebox in her hand. Inside it was a pair of ladies' brown lace-up brogues called HILDA. Without any shadow of a doubt, Goose was right. HILDA were putrid in the extreme. I wouldn't have worn them even if they were the last pair of shoes on Earth and I was the world champion of bad footwear. Goose replaced the lid, wedged them back on the shelf and then climbed down to pick up the fallen boxes.

'What have we got here? More pairs of HILDA in cream, navy and tan and . . .' she paused, lifting the lid of the fourth box. 'Hello? What are these?'

Inside the last box was a pair of flat black leather shoes the shape of ballet shoes and decorated all over with patterns of daisies. They were nice. In fact, they were blatantly ultra-nice. It's not often you can say such a thing about Sole Mates shoes.

'I've never seen those before,' I said. 'What are they called?'

Goose tilted the box to read the label. It was covered with dust as if it had been untouched for quite some time. 'ESMERELDA. And in size five. Which is perfect! They must be an old pair left over from a discontinued line or something.'

Goose looked at me thoughtfully. 'Do you reckon Dionne or Gina would notice if this one lonely pair of ESMERELDA shoes vanished?'

I laughed. 'I doubt it. And anyway, even if they did, they're hardly the Sherlock Holmes and Doctor Watson of the footwear world. It's just a pair of poxy shoes. And they are your size, after all. It's like they're *meant* for you, Goose.'

Goose nodded. 'Yeah, and do you know what? I reckon we'd be doing the shop a favour. Dionne did tell us to tidy up a bit, and there is so much junk out the back here that everything is a mess. It'd be good to make a little bit of room. It would give HILDA a bit more space on the shelf to stretch out and relax.'

'That's right,' I said. 'All the shoes would be happier and ESMERELDA would be going to a better life. You would be rescuing her from a fate of eternal obscurity in the stockroom of Sole Mates. Those shoes would be much better off on your feet.'

Goose nodded solemnly, slipped the shoes into her bag

and crushed the box with her heel. Placing her finger on her lips, she whispered, 'It is a far, far better thing that I do, than I have ever done.' And she grinned. I swear to God, I shall love that girl forever.

sOmetimes Life CaN reaLLY sLaP YOu iN the faCe

Goose is going out with Neil Adam. Neil Adam and Goose are going out. Together. Goose and Neil. Neil and Goose. How sly is that! It was Gareth Stingecombe who told me. I was walking home from school today when I heard all this huffing and puffing and running footsteps come charging up behind me. I stopped to turn around, and Gareth Stingecombe crashed right into the back of me, causing me to drop my premium-favourite genuine authentic Donna Karan shoulder bag, which is a totally essential school accessory even though it is too small to hold anything more than an MP3 player and a pen. My Donna Karan bounced right off my arm and landed in a puddle.

'Oh thanks, Gareth,' I said. 'I really wanted my genuine designer shoulder bag to be soaked in rainwater. That was really brilliant, thank you!'

Gareth looked a bit surprised for a second and then said, 'Phew! I thought I was in trouble. But you're right. It does look better now it's a bit scuffed up.'

I remembered then that Gareth Stingecombe doesn't do sarcasm. Take Beca Bowen's fifteenth birthday party, for instance. Almost everyone in Year 10 got invited to Beca's party, but by some weird trick of fate it was me that ended up dancing with Gareth Stingecombe. Gareth is a very good rugby player. He plays for our school and even plays for the Wales youth team sometimes, but this does not mean that he's a good dancer. He's not. I'd even go so far as to say that he's the worst dancer in the whole of Wales, if not the world. Gareth is quite a big lad, and I had to keep very alert in order to prevent him from amputating my toes with his size eleven feet. He can be quite sweet though so I kept these observations to myself. That was until he said, 'You need to loosen up a bit, Biggsy. It feels like I'm dancing with a stick of celery.'

I'd said, 'Oh I am sorry. It's just that it's not every day a girl gets to relive all her *Strictly Come Dancing* fantasies with Mr Sexy-Moves.'

Gareth had smiled and said, 'I suppose I am a bit of a sexy mover. Just relax and follow what I'm doing.'

Mr Wood once told us that Oscar Wilde[6] famously said that, 'Sarcasm is the lowest form of wit.' If this is true, it means that Gareth Stingecombe is completely off the witty scale, but only because he has never actually managed to get on to it. He is good at rugby though. And he does have a fairly nice face. So on that occasion I snogged him anyway.

I was thinking about all this while Gareth rubbed my bag dry against one of his colossal rugby thighs. Then he said, 'I know it's still ages away, but do you fancy coming with me to the upper-school disco at the end of term? The Sellotape Sistas are doing the music – it should be really good.'

---

[6] Oscar Wilde (1854–1900) was a very famous Irish writer whom everyone has heard of. Apparently.

I was not in a very good mood so I said, 'Not really. And besides, the Sellotape Sistas aren't all that fantastic.'

This is true. The Sellotape Sistas are actually just a couple of tragic teachers from the history department who do all our school discos and make us listen to random no-mark music from the ark, like Aretha Franklin and Stevie Wonder. For some reason though, everyone except me and Goose thinks they are really cool. Clearly mine and Goose's listening tastes are far more sophisticated and cutting edge than everyone else's. Goose even owns a CD by a band from Kortrijk which is a city in Belgium. She likes them because they are also called Goose.

Gareth Stingecombe looked a bit disappointed and said, 'Everyone else is going in couples. Hannah Roberts is going with Lee Fogel and Beca is going with my mate Spud. You'll be the odd one out, Biggsy.'

I said, 'That's OK, thank you. I'll go in a girl-power, man-magnet couple with Goose.'

And then Gareth said, 'You can't. Unless you want to be Goose's gooseberry, that is. Goose is going out with that posh boy who works in Suitably Booted.'

When he said these words, a funny thing happened to me.[7] It's not that I wasn't pleased for Goose because she's my best friend and I'm always pleased when something nice happens for her, but this time I went all hot and felt very very sick. I said, 'How do you know that?'

---

[7] Funny peculiar rather than funny ha ha.

Gareth Stingecombe said, 'It's only a wild guess, but I just saw her snogging his face off in the public garden.'

'You can't have done,' I said. 'Goose is in detention right now for giving Beethoven dreadlocks on the cover of her music book. She'd be walking home with me otherwise.' I put my hand up to my forehead. Nothing seemed to be making sense any more.

Gareth Stingecombe shrugged his shoulders. 'I say what I see, Biggsy. And I plainly saw Goose, just now, with her lips glued to the lips of that shoe-shop boy.'

This made me feel sicker than I can say. Neil Adam has got beautiful lips. I can't tell you how many times I've dreamed about kissing those lips myself. Just thinking about Goose getting in there first made me feel really bad. And she was probably wearing ESMERELDA when she did it as well. I got that painful feeling in my heart that I get when I can't breathe properly because I've been laughing too hard – only this time it felt one hundred per cent painful and no per cent funny. I suppose I probably sound like I'm a very awful person for not being pleased for the pair of them, but it wasn't my fault. It really wasn't. Hearing this piece of news regarding the good fortune of my best friend Goose – who was SUPPOSED to be in detention – and my dream lover Neil Adam caused a serious malfunction somewhere deep inside my brain.

It was like someone had switched off the lights and I was standing by myself in total darkness.

And then someone switched them back on again and I felt all dizzy and started laughing in a really weird way and said, 'Oh yeah, I remember Goose telling me about that now.'

And Gareth said, 'So will you come with me then?'

And I said, 'Sorry, Gaz. Maybe another time.'

And Gareth looked a bit sad and shrugged and walked off back towards the village, and I felt even worse.

iNNOCeNt fLOwers, DaNGerOus serPeNts aND the truth aBOut the COLOur GreeN

'I just can't believe it! Me and Neil are getting on so well. Last night I went round his house and he made me chocolate fondue. Chocolate fondue! How totally sophisticated is that? He is so unlike the scatty boys in our school. I can't believe we've only been together a week. It feels like we've known each other all our lives. Lottie, me and Neil are so compatible you wouldn't believe it.'

Goose has changed. Last night she was supposed to come round my house to watch *Free Willy 3* with me, but she rang up at the last minute and cancelled because she'd decided that she'd rather see *Slumber Party Massacre* with Mad Alien. I ended up watching *FW3* with my mum, who fell asleep twenty minutes after the opening credits. The old Goose would never have subjected me to such a tragic evening. The new Goose is a much more heartless individual. She keeps on dyeing her hair deliberately green and she is in love. She is also FANTASTICALLY BORING. Today in work she talked about Neil Adam the Mad Alien for twenty-six minutes solidly. I tried shifting around the shop to shake her off but she just kept following me. I also tried changing the subject.

'How many pairs of tights have you sold?'

'None yet. I'm so in love just at the moment that I can't really keep my mind on anything as trivial as a triple-pack of 10-denier American Tan. You'd understand if you were in the same situation.'

I have to be honest – this last comment was fairly annoying, but I am a very loyal friend and I like to think that I don't give up on people easily, so I tried again.

'How is recording going with the Tribe of Pixies?'

This time, for a minute or two at least, it worked and I managed to get Goose off the subject. She put down the duster she had been holding but not using for twenty-six minutes and frowned. 'Really rubbish. I'm getting severely stressed out with my backing band. Bill and James keep arguing all the time. I should have known that trying to create a CD masterpiece of grunge-folk-rock brilliance with them would be a complete drain of my artistic energy.'

Bill and James are Goose's musically gifted twin brothers. They are both child prodigies who have won countless competitions for playing the violin and the piano even though they are only in Year 8. Like me, they are also short for their age. This is why Goose always refers to them as pixies. As far as I can tell, they don't seem to mind. Despite the fact that Goose moans about them most of the time, Bill and James are actually quite cute. I haven't got any brothers or sisters who live in the same house as me, but if I did, I wouldn't mind a couple of pocket-sized musical geniuses like Bill and James. My older sister, Ruthie, is away at university in Aberystwyth studying archaeology. Ruthie is cool, but we aren't really on the same wavelength. I am fairly normal, whereas she has got a thing about damp, muddy holes and bits of broken pottery.

My baby brother, Caradoc, is five now and lives with my dad and his new wife in Wrexham so I don't get to see him very often. He might as well live in Oompa-Loompa land. Wrexham is miles away. Sometimes Caradoc doesn't even seem to be all that sure who I am, although I do try to talk to him on the phone now and again. It will be easier when he's a bit older, I suppose, and he knows how to text. Anyway, I guess what I'm trying to say is that if I was Goose, I'd be quite pleased to have Bill and James around. Sometimes being an only child at home can get a bit intense. Especially when your mum is a policewoman.

But at least I'd got Goose to change the subject.

I said, 'Are they still arguing about who's got the squeakiest voice?'

Goose wrinkled her nose and said, 'Yup, that kind of thing. Anyway, what are we talking about those little squirts for? Did I tell you what Neil said about the moment he knew for sure that he was totally in love with me? He said that when he bumped into me on the pavement when I first had my green hair, he just KNEW that I was the one for him. He said that . . .'

Luckily for me, I never got to hear what else the Mad Alien said because a customer came into the shop. It was a woman with three wailing little children who all needed their feet measuring. Asserting my authority as Head Saturday Girl, I instructed Goose to go and serve them. While she was busy, I disappeared out the back. Once safely out of view, I dragged the taller of the two stepladders around to the remotest corner of the stockroom and climbed up the top to sit and think for a bit.

There were a whole lot of questions whirring around my head. In fact, there were so many of them they didn't all seem to fit comfortably inside my brain. It felt like one more question could have caused my entire mind to blow a fuse.

AM I JEALOUS OF GOOSE – MY VERY BEST FRIEND?

DO I CARE?

WHO SHALL I GO TO THE UPPER SCHOOL DISCO WITH?

WILL I EVER FINISH MY ENGLISH COURSEWORK?

OH MY GOD!!

WHAT IF I'M JEALOUS OF NEIL ADAM?

DOES THAT MEAN I'M LESBOTIC????

PERHAPS I *SHOULD* GO OUT WITH GARETH STINGECOMBE?

HOW MUCH LONGER TILL LUNCHTIME?

DO I HONESTLY CARE ABOUT SELLING TIGHTS?

MAYBE *I* NEED GREEN HAIR

It was all beginning to give me a bit of headache.

In front of me was a pile of shoeboxes containing a ladies white slingback shoe called SADIE. Pulling one of the boxes out, I took a marker pen from my pocket and adjusted the label a bit.

these shoes are so blatantly

Sadie

White
Slingback court shoe
Man-made upper and sole

£17.99

Size 6

I put the marker pen back in my pocket and pushed the box to the back of the shelf where it couldn't be seen. My head felt a little bit better.

I stayed at the top of the ladder for another sixteen minutes before raised voices on the shop floor awakened my curiosity enough for me to abandon my perch. Downstairs, Goose was getting an ear-bashing from Dionne, who had only just surfaced from her office and was seeing Goose's latest application of bright green hair for the first time.

'I thought I told you that green hair was unacceptable for work. This is the second time I'm going to have to send you home on account of your personal appearance. If it happens again, Gail, I'll have to replace you with somebody else. Consider this your first and final warning.'

Dionne had gone a bit red in the face while she was saying

all this. Goose said, 'It was an accident. Honestly, Dionne. I didn't read the label properly. I thought that if you'd recently coloured your hair, you had to double the development time, not *halve* it. And anyway, I thought *emerald* was a red colour. I did, honestly. I'm really sorry.'

I happen to know for a fact that Goose knows full well what colour emerald is because she had a ring set with an emerald stone for her last birthday.

In the corner of the shop I laced up some trainers and watched quietly as Dionne sighed in an exasperated fashion and told Goose that she had two hours to sort her hair out. Goose promised that it wouldn't happen again, grabbed her bag from the stockroom and hurried out through the door. Crossing over to the window, I watched her as she ran up the street to her house via a short snog-stop at Suitably Booted.

In English we've been studying a play called *Macbeth*[8] by William Shakespeare, the creative-writing expert. Unfortunately I'm starting to see some similarities between that terrible woman Lady Macbeth and my so-called best friend, Goose. Both of them seem sweet and harmless on the outside but both are in fact driven by selfish greed to hurt other people in order to get what they want. It hurts me to say this. It really does. As any self-respecting scholar

---

[8] Although, Mr (or Mrs) Examiner, you know this already because you have already had the pleasure of reading my essay *Ten Good Reasons Why Lady Macbeth Needs Behaviour Counselling*.

of Mr Shakespeare knows, Lady Macbeth said that it was important to *look like an innocent flower but be the serpent underneath*, and this is EXACTLY what Goose is doing now. She is pretending her green hair was a mistake and she is pretending to be innocent of the deep emotional wound she has given me by stealing away my chance at happiness with Neil Adam. But actually her hair is as deliberate as the love bite that she is hiding beneath her polo-neck.

And whatever Mad Alien thinks, I don't think her green hair looks all that great.

In fact, it looks fairly putrid.

BuzziNG MY heaD Off

After Goose disappeared to de-greenify her hair, I started selling tights. American Tan. California Bronze. Large polka-dot. Small polka-dot. Fishnet. Seams and bows. If we had them, I sold them. I'm no mathematical genius, but the way I worked it out, it was simple. There was one prize and three Saturday girls. That meant my chances of winning were one in three. When you compare this to the odds of winning the lottery – one in thirty-three zillion – this is definitely quite favourable. Not even the reappearance of Gina worried me. Dionne had stated very clearly that this was a competition for Saturday *girls*, and it doesn't take supersonic specs to see that Gina is *way* past ever qualifying in this category – even if she does have the fashion sense of a Teletubby. In short,

Opponent Number 1

Side Pony →

bling →

Gina = too old.

Which left me up against Emily and Goose. Elvis Presley in the public garden has more chance of ever selling any tights than Emily, and he spends most of his time asleep on a bench. Don't get me wrong – Emily is a good and sensible person, but she lacks the necessary drive and ambition to succeed in the cut-throat world of retail commerce. Sometimes a little bit of nastiness is necessary if you want to get ahead. In short,

Opponent Number 2

doesn't speak to boys

Emily = too nice.

So that meant that the competition was really just between me and Goose. And although Goose has already proved that she is more than capable of enough nastiness to rival Lady

Macbeth, I knew she couldn't win if I maximized on my two-hour head start. In short,

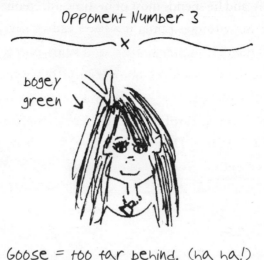

Opponent Number 3

bogey
green ↓

Goose = too far behind. (ha ha!)

Which meant that *I* was actually the only serious contender in this contest. And those REALLY ARE good odds. To be honest though,

IT DIDN'T MATTER WHO WON SO LONG AS IT WASN'T GOOSE.

With this thought burning a hole in my head, I prowled the shop floor and began my campaign. I was quite buzzed up. I couldn't think about anything except winning. *I* wanted to win. I HAD to win. Without even needing to work out a strategy, my mind switched on to autopilot and began to take me step by step through a masterclass in tights-selling brilliance.

Step One: **Send Emily out the back to hunt for a pair of ESMERELDAs in size five for an imaginary customer called Audrey.** (This would keep Emily out of the way for a while, because the only pair of ESMERELDAs I've ever seen now live under Goose's bed.)

Step Two: **Rush forward and approach all customers before Gina gets to them. Overwhelm them with helpfulness and charm and fetch from the back whatever shoes they want.** (Gina couldn't match my speed and agility on the shop floor because one side of her head is heavier than the other and this gives her severe steering problems.)

Step Three: **When customers are at till, say 'Oh, aren't these ANGIE court shoes lovely! I think they'd look totally tremendous with a pair of 10-denier silk-finish midnight tights.'** (Or something similar.)

Sometimes it all worked. Sometimes it didn't.

As the morning wore on, I got more confident. In fact,

I started to feel so confident that I became convinced I could sell ANYTHING. I started to say stuff like, 'Wow, these NICOLE high heels are gorgeous. I think they're just screaming out to be teamed with a pair of foxy black freaky fishnets.'

Then when Goose returned with brown hair and added a real sense of urgency to my tights-selling operation, I asked Gina if I could stand on the pavement outside the shop so that I'd be able to take maximum advantage of any passing trade, and after a bit of humming and hah-ing, she agreed. I filled a basket with tights and went outside and started approaching people in the street. And I was doing SO well. I must have shifted at least twenty pairs. But then something very weird happened. The Pixie Twins, Bill and James, turned up and Bill was carrying Goose's guitar.

They were blatantly up to something, and if I hadn't been so busy pretending not to be interested, I'd have had a good stare. Instead, I kept my head turned in the other direction and went right on shouting, 'Give your husband some sexy nights – buy a triple-pack of budget tights!'

A few moments later, out of the corner of my eye, I saw Goose appear and place a basket of tights next to her on the pavement. She took the guitar from Bill and then, pulling a plectrum from her pocket, she picked out an opening E chord and began to SING to the passing public.

How completely random is that?

Her song was kind of slow and bluesy and went like this.

I woke up this morning
And my tights were a fright
So wrinkled and crumpled
Like I'd been in a fight.

Several people smiled and stopped on the pavement to listen.

So I got me down to Sole Mates
With one-fifty in my hands
And now I'm the proud new owner
Of a pair of American Tans!

Goose's rapidly growing audience began to laugh. Goose pouted back at them, cleared her throat and raised her right arm high in the air, plectrum proudly aloft. Then, swinging her arm down dramatically, she tossed back her hair and began to strum very very fast.

Cos they've got tights in every size,
Fishnet and woolly and striped.
Yeah, tights for skinny and fat girls
And for businessmen in disguise.
So get your tights in every size
If your old ones are laddered and lined
And wearing them makes you feel minging

And leaves you with tears in your eyes.
Tights in every size . . .
Tights ·in every size . . .

The ending to Goose's song was lost in a spontaneous round of applause. I stood by and watched as the shoppers of Whitchurch Village went mad for her. Goose grinned and gave a small curtsy. A fat woman in a blue anorak said, 'Well, love, seeing as how you've given us all a bit of a laugh, I'll have two pairs of lightweight tan tights in extra large. Thank you very much.'

Another woman came forward holding a five-pound note and said, 'Go on, love – I'll have a couple of pairs as well.'

I faded into fuzzy nothingness as Goose sold almost every single box of tights in her basket. Then, when the crowd of shoppers had dispersed, she turned to me and said, 'Right, that's my lot. At least Dionne and Gina can't say I didn't make an effort.' And she went inside the shop and Bill and James disappeared up Merthyr Road with her guitar and I was left standing on the pavement with my almost-full basket of tights. And then it started to rain.

Around me, people hurried past with their hoods up or dashed into shop doorways. Everyone was in a hurry to get indoors. Except me. I didn't go inside. I couldn't. I couldn't face Goose. I couldn't face the fact that she always seemed to be better than me at EVERY SINGLE THING IN THE ENTIRE WORLD. So I just stayed where I was on the pavement. It was now raining pretty heavily and my semi-permanent hair colour, Melody Classic Ash, was running off my head a bit and causing brown-tinged raindrops to roll down my face and make watery-brown stains on the shoulders of my white blouse.

Goose popped her head around the shop door and shouted, 'Lottie, are you coming inside?'

I said, 'Umm . . . in a bit. I'm testing my hair dye to see if it's waterproof.'

Goose shrugged and disappeared back into the shop, but before she went she gave me a funny look. A minute or so later Gina's ponytail and half her face appeared in the doorway and she said, 'Lottie, love, you coming inside? It's raining, innit.'

She must think I'm stupid or something. I said, 'Yes, I do know that, thank you, Gina.'

'Well, the boxes of tights are getting wet, innit.'

I had forgotten all about the tights. I said, 'Can you lend me an umbrella?'

Gina looked a bit uncertain about this, but after a second she disappeared inside briefly and then resurfaced with a huge green umbrella shaped like a frog with eyes sticking out of the top of it. I looked at it doubtfully. She said, 'Come in when you're ready, love. But remember, no competition is worth catching pneumonia over.'

I stood in the rain, holding the gigantic frog umbrella. Across the road, Keith Bright was waving at me and had a rare smile on his furry face. I narrowed my eyes and gave him

my very best Stare of Death
but he didn't seem
particularly bothered
by it.

And suddenly I was so
annoyed about, well, everything,
that before I could stop myself,
I shouted,

'You're all such a bunch of virgins!'

I have no idea why I said it or who I was saying it to. I just felt really wound up. One of the few remaining shoppers who hadn't disappeared out of the rain paused on the pavement and tilted her umbrella to look at me. She had grey hair and looked about fifty. She said, 'I don't think so, love.' She raised her wrist to look at her watch. 'I last had sex about eight hours ago. And you?'

'Urgghh! Shut up!' I said and went really red. The woman laughed and carried on walking.

Cars drove slowly by and sent up spray from the puddles. It struck me how busy the world was.

The last time I went up to Wrexham to see Caradoc and my dad, and Sally his new wife, Caradoc had been playing with a toy kaleidoscope which shifted thousands of tiny red and green grains into millions of star-shaped patterns, each one a little different from the last. Looking round me, I realized that Merthyr Road was the same. No picture taken of it in one moment could be exactly the same as the next.

And in the midst of all this, the one thing that was not moving was my body. I was standing, stockstill, outside Sole Mates, with the rain running off the edges of my giant frog umbrella.

But don't be fooled. My body might have been motionless, but my brain was doing this:

Whizzing around and around like a tornado – and trying to figure out how I could sell more tights than Goose.

And that was when I saw Elvis Presley. He was half walking, half dancing towards me through the rain. In his hand, he was holding a plastic toy microphone – the sort that makes your voice echo a little bit and which is quite good fun for about five minutes when you're five years old – and into it he was singing, 'You were always on my mind' in this deep booming, dead authentic Welsh Elvis voice, and the few people still on the streets were laughing and patting him on the back as he passed and telling him how good he was and how he should be on *Stars in Their Eyes*. And then my head stopped doing this . . .

and did this
instead:

I ran up to meet him, still holding the frog umbrella and the basket of tights, and asked him if he could help me. And it just goes to show that you should ALWAYS BE POLITE TO PEOPLE, no matter how unusual or odd or scatty their personal circumstances may seem because you never know when the boot might be on the other foot and they might be needed to lend *you* a helping hand. And me and Elvis stood side by side outside Sole Mates sharing the frog umbrella and

I joined him in his song, except we changed the words a bit so they went like this:

> *Maybe I didn't wear you*
> *Quite as proudly as I could*
> *Maybe I put some holes in you*
> *A bit more often than I should*
> *Smelly tights*
> *That I should have thrown away*
> *But I never had the time.*
> *You were always on my thighs*
> *You were always on my thighs.*

We sang our song as loud as we could, and together, as the sun came back out, we sold every single one of those boxes of cheap tights.

. . . aND theN feeLiNG tOtaLLY rOBBeD

I like English. I really do. The other day Goose asked me how I was getting on with my personal writing project and I told her that so far I've spent eleven hours on it and written approximately fourteen thousand words. You should have seen her face when I said that. She looked like this.[9] ———▷

---

[9] This is a quick inkpen interpretation of MY FAVOURITE EVER painting. The original is by a Norwegian artist called Edvard Munch and I've spent the last two months copying it for my art project. Mr Spanton, my art teacher, says I should start thinking about drawing something else soon because I'm beginning to make his nerves bad.

I could tell that she was pretty freaked out. She went really pale and blotchy and said, 'Blimey, Lottie. I've only spent twenty minutes on mine so far and I think I've written about eighty words. Are you sure Mr Wood expects us to write that much?'

I said, 'Well, it is an important piece of work, Goose. You don't want to let Mad Alien distract you from your GCSEs, you know. GCSEs provide the key to many future career doorways.'

Goose looked even more freaked out when I said this and asked me if I'd spent as long over my maths coursework, and I was forced to admit that no, I hadn't.

Mind you, even though I like English, I don't like all aspects of it. Take poetry, for instance. I don't understand the point of poetry at all. I reckon that if you have something to say, it's best to just say it in as clear a way as possible so that everyone can understand what you mean. I told this to Mr Wood, who is making us read some really random poetry at the moment by a poet called Stevie Smith who, bizarrely, is actually a woman. When I'd finished getting it all off my chest, Mr Wood sighed for a moment and then said, 'One day, Charlotte, you will read a piece of poetry and it will speak directly to your heart as if the poet had you specifically in mind when they were writing. And you will be so moved with emotion that you will cherish that poem always and carry it with you forever in your memory and then, Charlotte, you will understand the point of poetry. Trust me.'

Mr Wood does speak a colossal amount of crap sometimes, he honestly does.[10]

Mind you, nothing that Mr Wood has ever said can compare with the almighty crap that came out of Dionne and Gina's mouths after I won the tights-selling competition last Saturday. It was a moment of unrivalled disappointment and even though I might never find a poem that I will want to carry around forever in my head, I know that I'll live to be colossally ancient before I forget how well and truly stitched up I was over the tights.

On Saturday, just before the shop closed, me, Goose and Emily were called into Dionne's office. I don't want to sound arrogant, but I was feeling so fantastically confident that I'd been skipping around as perky as a party popper all afternoon. This is quite unusual for me on a rainy Saturday in Sole Mates. Although recently, I admit, I've had a tremendous amount of energy in me, I really have. I hardly even need to sleep much, which is really handy because I've been up most nights working on this piece of coursework. Like I am now. In fact, at this precise moment, it is 3.07 a.m.

Anyway, Dionne sat in her chair and, in between mouthfuls of custard slice, told us the sales figures for the tights. Next

---

[10] Mr Wood, on the off chance that you *do* bother to read this before you send it off to the examiner, please don't take this comment personally. I think you are a very good teacher but it's important for me to retain a balanced perspective. Otherwise the examiner might think I'm trying to win marks by phoney flattery.

to her, Gina stood with her arms folded and her head on one side (because of the weight of her ponytail) and listened (because she is nosy).

'OK, in third place with a sum total of six boxes of tights sold is Emily.'

So Emily came last. Big shocker!

'And in second place with twenty-six boxes sold is . . . Goose.'

I looked across triumphantly at Goose and shrugged my shoulders in a way which meant

1. *Never mind, at least you tried.*

and

2. *I've won!!! Ha Ha.*

To my annoyance, Goose didn't seem bothered at all. She just laughed and said, 'Even I can't compete with Elvis Presley. How many tights did Lottie sell and what does she win?'

And I added, 'Yes, what *do* I win?'

Dionne said, 'You sold an amazing forty-one boxes. Close your eyes.' So I did, and she put something small and flat into my hands and when I opened my eyes again I was looking at this.

THE SOLE MATES
SHOP FLOOR SOUNDS CD

25 modern pop favourites
(not by the original artists)

I stared at the cover for a second, and then I flipped it over and looked at the other side. On the back was printed the entire track listing but I only got as far as reading the details for the first song.

1 'Angels' (Robbie Williams) performed by the Phil Fernandez All Stars.

Next to me, Goose started to laugh. I frowned and put the CD down on Dionne's desk and said, 'Is this a joke?'

Dionne cast a sideways glance at Gina and gave her a wink. 'I promised you a prize and there it is.'

I took a really deep breath and then I said, 'Do you mean to say that I've run about all day trying to sell your stupid cheap tights just for one of these awful CDs? Is that seriously what you're trying to tell me?'

Up until this point Gina had been keeping fairly quiet for once, but now she pulled the type of face that I'd pull if someone shoved a liver-and-cow-tongue sandwich under my nose. Then she piped up with, ''Ow ungrateful! In my day, Missy Biggs, we'd be pleased to get any type of present, innit. You lot today don't know you're born.'

Before I could stop myself I said, 'Yes, but I think you'll find that we've learned to stand up straight and walk on two legs since then.' And I threw the CD down on the floor and stamped on it. The CD case cracked and the disc went skidding across the carpet.

Dionne looked at me long and hard. It wasn't exactly a Stare of Death but it was fairly close. After a moment or so she said, 'I suggest you go home now, Lottie, and have a think about the way you've just spoken to me and Gina and come back next week when you've calmed down and are ready to apologize.' And then I felt Goose take hold of my arm and heard her say, 'She didn't mean it. I think she's just a bit stressed out at the moment.' And I kind of sniffed and nodded and half apologized (but not quite) and followed Goose and Emily out into the stockroom.

When Emily had gone and me and Goose were alone, I took my bag from off the hook and unzipped the top. It is important to point out that I don't use my genuine authentic Donna Karan shoulder bag for work, I use my Nike backpack instead because I need something big enough to hold my sandwiches. At school this is not an issue because I get a dinner ticket. Anyway, after unzipping my backpack, I pulled a shoebox from off the shelf, emptied its contents straight into my bag and then put the box back exactly where I'd found it. Goose said, 'What are you doing?'

I said, 'I'm rescuing some LAYLA ballet pumps in size four. I think that's the least I deserve for singing with Elvis in the rain today in aid of Sole Mates retail profits.'

Goose looked a bit shocked and said, 'Do you like LAYLA then? I think they're putrid.'

I shrugged my shoulders. 'I don't care. Dionne promised a prize so she needs to pay up. She can't just fob me off with some stupid CD from head office. That's not fair.'

And then I laughed and emptied the contents of another shoebox into my bag and this time I didn't even bother to look to see what I was rescuing. I just took it anyway.

trYiNG NOt tO CrY whiLe DrawiNG aN amOeBa

Something that Goose said to me yesterday has been playing on my mind a bit. It was during double science and we were sat on those high stools in the chemistry lab trying not to die of severe boredom while Mr Thomas drew random blobs on the whiteboard that looked like this:

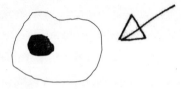

All the science geeks in our class were busy copying down the random blobs but I was too busy playing hangman with Goose to bother. Usually we have quite a giggle doing this, but Goose's Hangman was fairly obvious, to tell the truth. I only needed a few more letters to win the game but I was deliberately guessing wrong ones just to avoid uttering out loud anything so dreadfully horrific.

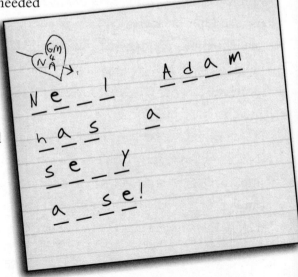

I'd just guessed a Z when Mr Thomas stopped what he was doing and said, 'Lottie, are you paying attention?'

I said, 'No, but I *was* listening though.'

Mr Thomas gave me a dirty look and then he said, 'So let me just get this clear. You *are* listening to what I'm saying but you're *not* paying any attention to it. Is that right?'

My head went blank. To be honest, I wasn't really sure whether I should answer yes or no. After a few edgy seconds I said, 'Yes, I think so.'

Mr Thomas gave a deep sigh and looked at the ceiling. Then he said, 'Have you learnt anything this lesson?'

And I said, 'Ye-es.'

Mr Thomas seemed blatantly unconvinced. In a very irritated voice, he said, 'Do you know what this is then?' And he tapped the blob he had drawn on the whiteboard and gave me a particularly nasty look. I hate being put on the spot. I really do. I've never performed very well under pressure. As you might have noticed already, pressure makes me say flippant things. My brain goes into panic overload and then the resulting stress builds up the pressure inside my head, which forces my mouth to open and something unhelpful to pop out of it. I looked at the blob on the board and said, 'Is it a fried egg?'

Mr Thomas shook his head very slowly and deliberately. 'No, Lottie,' he said. 'It isn't. It's an amoeba. An amoeba is a single-celled creature which constantly changes shape and can only be seen with the aid of a microscope. And quite frankly, this amoeba that I've just drawn here has more chance of doing well in a GCSE science exam than you have, if you don't start listening to what I'm saying and do some work for once.' And then he started raving on some more about how I don't listen enough and about how it won't be long until I have exams and stuff, and to be honest he was actually quite angry with me and his rant went on for almost four minutes, and I really didn't want to hear it because I happen to believe that I could probably pass any science exam I ever want to because, after all, it can't be that hard writing about the sex life of a plant, can it? So I just sat there patiently and gave him the most sincere *I'm hearing you* face that I have.

By the time he'd finished moaning on at me and gone back to drawing blobs, I was feeling a bit cheesed off. Goose gave me a sympathetic look and whispered, 'Sorry, Lotts. I wanted to tell you it was an amoeba, but Thommo was giving me the evil eyeball so I couldn't.'

I said, 'Well, thanks for nothing!'

Goose went a bit quiet then and for

a few minutes both of us just sat there on our high stools, ignoring each other and drawing amoebas in our exercise books.

After what felt like ages Goose said, 'Is something wrong, Lottie?'

I said, 'No. Apart from having my ear severely chewed off for four hours by Mr Thomas, everything is perfectly fine, thank you very much.'

Goose bit her lip, sighed and said, 'It's just that you've been acting really weird recently.'

I shifted on my stool and looked up at Goose's face. She looked genuinely concerned and actually rather upset. This made me feel a bit bad. After all, it's not totally her fault that Neil Adam fancied her instead of me. I shifted some more on my stool and said, 'It's OK, Goose, honest. I've just been in a bit of a dodgy mood recently, that's all.'

Goose raised her eyebrows. 'Do you think you're having an existential moment?' She smiled a bit and added, 'You'll be writing poetry and dreaming about going to live in Iceland and stuff next.'

I thought about this for a second and then I said, 'Not really Goose. I can't say that I've ever thought about going to Iceland. For a start, I don't really like frozen food all that much. I'm just in a bad mood.'

And all of a sudden I got this big buzzy rush of giggles and I started laughing so hard that Gareth Stingecombe on the next table looked over and said, 'Biggsy's off her blinking head again,' and then he winked and blew me a kiss, which actually made me shut up fairly quickly. But Goose wasn't laughing at all. For some reason she was just sitting there looking at me with this worried expression on her face. And then she took hold of my hand and squeezed it and said, 'Well, so long as that's all it is. If ever you need someone to talk to about anything, you know you can always talk to me.'

And it was a real relief to feel close to Goose again, and I smiled and squeezed her hand back and then we both picked up our pens and started drawing the fried-egg diagrams that Mr Thomas was putting up on the board. And all the time, I was still sort of quietly laughing to myself about the Iceland joke even though I knew it was blatantly a very pathetic joke indeed. But the truth is, I didn't want to stop laughing because, all of a sudden, I had this terrifying feeling that if I did stop, I'd start crying instead, and I just couldn't have handled that in the middle of Mr Thomas's double-science lesson.

trYiNG NOt tO LauGh whiLe resCuiNG a Giraffe

Gareth Stingecombe was waiting for me when I walked out of school at the end of the day. He was sitting on the wall of the graveyard, eating a chocolate bar and fiddling with his iPod. When he saw me he shoved the remaining half of the chocolate bar in his mouth and jumped down off the wall. I carried on walking and pretended I hadn't seen him. It's not that I don't like Gareth or anything, it's just that after all the aggravation with Mr Thomas and his amoebas, I didn't fancy talking to anyone all that much – not even Goose who had got herself a detention for performing an unbleeped version of a 50 Cent song in her music lesson. It hadn't been a very good day.

Gareth said, 'All right, Biggsy? You seemed off your head in science.'

I stopped walking and stared at him. I couldn't exactly remember what had gone wrong in science or why Mr Thomas had got so mad at me. I said, 'If you don't mind, Gaz, I'd rather not talk about it right now.'

Gareth Stingecombe shrugged. I started to walk on again, and Gareth walked alongside me. I didn't say so to him but, actually, it felt quite nice to have his company. Instead of turning right towards my house, I crossed over Church Road and began making my way towards the shops in Merthyr Road. My mum never gets home from work until gone six and I really didn't feel in the mood to be by myself.

Gareth said, 'Tell you what, Biggsy, how about I buy you a cup of tea or something in that fancy cafe over there?'

I looked to where he was pointing and saw that he meant the Dragon Coffee House. I gave a half-smile and said, 'It's not that fancy, actually, Gareth. Me and Goose go in there all the time.'

Gareth went a bit red. 'You're hard work, Biggsy – you know that?'

I immediately felt awful. I can be an awkward witch sometimes, I know I can. It's probably what comes of having beige hair for most of my life. I wanted to say sorry to Gareth but I didn't really know how to without getting all intense, so instead, I linked my arm through his, gave him a big smile and said, 'I had a difficult day at the office, darling.'

Gareth looked surprised and went even redder. It made him look seriously cute and a bit sensitive. But then he went all tough again and said, 'You're telling me, Biggsy! You've had a face like a dropped pie all day.'

I started to laugh. Gareth laughed as well and seemed to relax a bit. I think he quite liked having my arm hooked through his. I quite liked it too. As we arrived at the coffee house he said, 'So are you absolutely definitely sure you don't want to come to the end-of-term disco with me? Say no now, Biggsy, and you could spend the rest of your life kicking yourself.'

I hesitated, my hand on the door of the cafe. Gareth looked at me, waiting for me to say something, and when I didn't he began to look a touch annoyed. I started to panic then and this stern voice inside my head said, 'DON'T BE SO RUDE, CHARLOTTE! GIVE HIM AN ANSWER.' I opened my mouth to say something, but nothing at all came out. It was as if I'd completely forgotten how to speak. And it wasn't as if I was struggling because I didn't know how to let him down gently or anything like that. That wasn't the problem at all. Because right there and then, at that particular moment in the whole history of time, I WANTED to go to the disco with him, I REALLY DID, but there was this other question which had just broken out in my head and that was:

How *on EARTH* was I supposed to know if I'd STILL feel like going in a few weeks' time?

Because right then I wasn't sure about what I felt like doing from one second to the next. Right at that moment I wasn't actually very sure about anything at all. Not even why I was alive. It's not a nice feeling to have, believe me.

And just when I thought things couldn't get any weirder, I saw Neil Adam and Emily inside the Dragon Coffee House.

'So do you want to come with me to this disco or not?' asked Gareth.

What was Neil Adam doing in there with Emily?

And I couldn't concentrate on ANYTHING that Gareth was saying because the inside of my brain had gone completely like this:

and I found I was laughing. Like little hiccups at first and then a bit more and a bit more until it was finally a big full-on howling belly laugh and I was having difficulty standing up straight.

Gareth Stingecombe turned a deep beetroot purple and then said, 'Oh, forget it!' and stomped off down Merthyr Road.

I watched him walk off, getting further and further away from me, and I wanted to call him back and apologize and try to explain about the black hole in my brain, but I couldn't because I was laughing too hard to get any words out and, to be honest, it was all beginning to make my heart hurt. And then I turned back to Neil Adam and Emily inside the coffee shop and I stopped laughing. Instantly. One second it was

Haha haha haha

and the next it was ## Ha h☹

Because they were snogging shamelessly over what looked like double choco-mochaccinos. Neil Adam and Emily. Emily and Neil Adam. Emily, who doesn't talk to boys! I spun around so that my back was facing the window. I didn't want either of them to see me. For a few minutes I stood completely still, staring at the traffic on the road and not daring to move in case I attracted any attention to myself. And then, when my heart had slowed down and I was feeling a bit calmer, I said to myself, 'Maybe I got that wrong. Maybe it was *Goose* in there with him. Maybe she got let out early from the music detention. Or maybe that's not Neil Adam at all. Just someone who looks amazingly like him.' So I turned around, ever so slowly, to have another look and

OH MY GOD

it *was* them! Neil Adam and Emily. In a compromising situation.

I turned and started walking very quickly down Merthyr Road. Neither of them had seen me; that I *was* sure about. In all honesty, it's difficult to notice people staring at you through a cafe window when you've got your eyes shut and your tongue twisted round someone else's tonsils. I kept on walking, and all the time I was walking I was thinking HOW AM I GOING TO TELL GOOSE?

And I couldn't think of an answer so I just kept right on walking until I realized that lots of cars were beeping their horns at me and I was actually one hundred metres up in the air with four lanes of fast-moving traffic whizzing right by my left ear. I stopped then. I'd gone a bit dizzy. Somehow I'd walked on to the flyover – and although it's got a narrow pavement, I don't think you're actually supposed to use it. Which was probably why all the cars were tooting their horns at me.

Holding my breath, so I didn't pass out from all the traffic fumes, I carefully did an about-turn and began walking back to Whitchurch. My head was all over the place. It reminded me of a doll my sister, Ruthie, had once found in a jumble sale and given to me when I was a little girl. It was made of hard plastic and had a massive head and a tiny body. The tiny body was attached to the massive head by a cord, and when you held on to the head, pulled the body as far as you could and then let go, the cord and body wound back in and the doll spoke. She said loads of different things and all of them in an increasingly manic American voice. Stuff like 'That's quite a stretch!' Or, 'Whoops, I lost my head for a moment!'

Or 'My feet are moving closer!' It was my most favourite toy ever! Something about that massive head and that tiny body and that bonkers American voice just used to make me laugh and laugh. I played with it all the time, until one sad day I pulled the body too hard and the cord snapped, leaving nothing but a decapitated head in my hand.

I haven't thought about that mad doll for years, but I was thinking about it as I walked back to Whitchurch from the flyover after seeing Neil Adam and Emily with their faces stuck together. And all I could hear inside my head was this mad American voice saying stuff like:

Whoops, I lost my head for a moment!

and

I'm falling apart. Oh no!

It was all very random.

The next thing I knew, I was in the Pound Shop. I don't

know why I'd gone in there because it's a very scatty shop full of very scatty items and most of the customers who go in there have still got their slippers on. But somehow I was in there, and I was walking up and down the aisles just staring at stuff when I came to a stop in front of a shelf full of small cuddly giraffes. They looked like this.[11]

They were actually quite cute and not bad quality really, considering they only cost a pound. So I stood there in the Pound Shop, looking into the brown button eyes of this stuffed giraffe and, I swear to God, it felt like the toy was talking to me. First, my mad doll and now this one-pound giraffe!

The giraffe said, 'Lottie, why don't you give me to Goose? I'm dead cute and she's going to need some serious cheering up when she finds out what a total toad that minging Mad Alien is.'

And I thought about it and then I said, 'You're right! Hang on, I'll just get my purse out of my authentic Donna Karan shoulder bag.'

---

[11] Dear Mr (or Mrs) Examiner, I would just like to point out that although art is my favourite subject, I am not particularly skilled in animal portraiture.

I didn't say this out loud, of course. I said it telepathically. I'm not a maniac.

And then the giraffe said, 'Oh, don't bother with that. Just rescue me. It'll be more funny if you rescue me.'

I looked up and down the aisle, but I couldn't see any staff about. It was nearly five o'clock and it seemed that the only two people working were both at the tills dealing with the last-minute rush of customers who were queuing up to pay for their garden gnomes and clothes pegs and the other types of stuff you get in a shop where everything costs a pound.

I picked the giraffe up from the shelf.

'Quick, Lottie. Put me in your bag,' he said.

I looked at my authentic Donna Karan shoulder bag. It already had my purse, a biro, my mascara and my MP3 player inside it. It was full to bursting. There wasn't any room for anything else. There especially wasn't any room for a giraffe.

Taking a deep breath, I held the giraffe casually by its neck and let it swing down by the side of my leg. And then I slowly continued wandering through the aisles of the pound shop pretending to browse the gnomes and the clothes pegs as I went. I don't know if you've ever tried to rescue a giraffe from a pound shop before, but I have to say there was really something hysterically funny about it. It was even funnier than being moaned at by Mr Thomas for seventeen hours. It was so funny that I was actually having a hard job trying not to laugh. But I knew that if I was to save the giraffe, it was really important that I didn't start acting all peculiar so I kept my face perfectly still and continued casually wandering up and down the aisles, swinging my giraffe by its neck until I casually just wandered right out of the shop. And then when I was out on the pavement, I shouted,

'Whoops, I lost my head for a moment!'

and laughed so much that I nearly fell over. It was definitely the best moment I'd had all day. I almost went straight back inside the shop so that I could rescue another giraffe for Gareth.

When I got home my mum still wasn't back from work. I put my rescued giraffe on the kitchen table and got my dinner out of the fridge and put it in the microwave. The note on the fridge from my mum said that it needed six minutes. I turned the timer and then I sat down and looked at my giraffe. Inside the microwave, my cottage pie was going round and round and starting to glisten a bit. In front of me, on the table, my giraffe wasn't doing anything. One of its legs was a bit shorter than the others and was causing it to wonk. And it looked like one of its button eyes was soon going to fall off. To be honest it was not a very good giraffe. It was actually fairly tragic.

I sat for a while and just stared at my giraffe. My cottage pie carried on whirring around inside the microwave and then I heard the ping that meant that it was ready. But all of a sudden I didn't feel hungry. I picked up the giraffe and headed to my bedroom. I didn't want to give Goose a tragic giraffe that was on the wonk. I especially didn't want to give her something I hadn't paid for. I opened the door of my wardrobe, threw the giraffe inside and then closed the door again.

a Brief wOrD aBOut the tOtaLLY raNDOm Nature Of LOve aND POetrY

Mr (or Mrs) Examiner, I know that the middle of my Creative Writing Coursework is not exactly the best place to share my thoughts on the utterly bizarre and freakish topics of love (yuck!!!) and poetry (yawn) but I'm going to anyway. I have to. I need to share my thoughts with somebody, and you are the only person who will listen to me. Goose is currently in a state of emotional derangement and any mention of the word love is likely to tip her right over the edge. My mum is no good either. During the week she's hardly ever in, and during the weekend I hardly ever am. My sister, Ruthie, is only interested in muddy bits of broken pottery. She is not really the sort of person who would understand. And besides that, she's in Aberystwyth.

The thing is, as far as I can tell, love and poetry are pretty much the same thing. Let me explain. Firstly, they are both what Mr Wood would describe as *abstract nouns*. This means that you can't really touch them, hold them, draw them or collect them but they're both still kind of just *there,* if you know what I mean. Sort of like period pain. Or detention.

Secondly, you can't have one without the other. When people are in love they write poems, and when you read that poetry you learn about how blatantly random the whole concept of love is. We have been doing a whole load of poetry in school lately because it's Mr Wood's favourite thing. Sometimes he reads a poem to us and then, when he's finished, he takes off his specs and just sits there at his desk for a moment, waving the specs in front of him while he stares into space and mutters, 'Wonderful. How perfectly wonderful!' Clearly the inside of his head is a very freaky place. Anyway, from what I have read so far, I estimate that probably at least half the poems ever written are soppy love poems. I happen to know that the correct term for these is *sonnets*. Now, you would assume that a sonnet would be a happy and uplifting poem because the person who wrote it was so madly in love and generally feeling fairly good about life . . .

WRONG!!!!!!!!

Poets – and writers of sonnets in particular – are the most messed-up bunch of people who ever walked this earth. Most of their poems are full of very strange and, frankly, quite useless questions like:

'How do I love thee? Let me count the ways.'

and

'Shall I compare thee to a summer's day?'

and all that usually happens is that the poet whines on for fourteen lines about how terrible they feel and then, when you get to the end, you find out that the person they fancied is actually God. Or somebody else equally unavailable. It's all totally pointless and just a little bit weird.

So, if being in love causes people to write such drippy crap, you would think that the sensible thing to do would be:

NEVER to fall in love
and
NOT to read any poetry.

Unfortunately this is not easily done. Mr Wood told me AGAIN today that I HAVE to study poetry because it's ON THE CURRICULUM. I told him quite bluntly that this means that the curriculum is responsible for a shocking waste of my time. I could be learning something useful and interesting like how to talk Russian or how to train a baby guide dog, but instead I'm forced to fill up my head with the weird words of Stevie Smith. She, actually, doesn't write about love but she does write stuff like this:

> *Aloft,*
> *In the loft,*
> *Sits Croft;*
> *He is soft.*

I have no idea why.

As for falling in love, you may try to steer clear of it, but it creeps up and gets you in the end. And when it does, the results are messy. I speak from experience. Not personal experience. I am as yet to find any boy, other than Gareth Stingecombe, who is not completely put off by my dodgy nose – and I'm steering well clear of him right now because the LAST thing I need is my own total eclipse of the heart. However, I *can* speak from observing the CATASTROPHIC impact that love has had upon my best friend, Goose. Goose has been a wreck ever since she found out about Evil Emily's dirty affair with Emperor Ming. It wasn't me that told her. I know, as her best friend, I should have done, but it wasn't exactly a topic of conversation I fancied. I'm sure that sounds selfish but I just couldn't bear to witness the total meltdown of Goose's happiness.

The day after The Cafe Scandal, I got the bus into town or somewhere instead of going to school. I couldn't face Goose. I didn't know what to say to her. I didn't actually know what to say to anyone. I just wanted to be on my own. But then Saturday came and we were all back in the shop. Emily was keeping a low profile and looking a bit edgy. I noticed that she'd started wearing red lipstick, probably for Mad Alien's benefit. When Goose was out the back getting some DWAYNE trainers in a size ten, I whispered, 'Nice lipstick, Emily. Matches your eyes.' Emily's face went red then as well, and she moved over to the furthest corner of the shop and started picking up bits of fluff from underneath the men's slip-on fixtures.

And I was really agitated so I started taking all the laces out of all of the shoes. I'd been doing this for about twenty minutes when a man tapped me on the arm and said, 'Excuse me. A young lady went out the back to fetch me a size ten training shoe some time ago and she hasn't come out again.'

It took me a moment to register what he had just said. I'd been miles away. I'd been thinking about Gareth Stingecombe in his rugby kit, for some random reason.

'So?' I said.

'So will you go and see where she's got to for me?'

The man was starting to look a bit fed up so I headed for the stockroom. Out the back it was deathly quiet. All I could hear was some putrid smoochy love song coming faintly from a radio in Dionne's office. There was no sign of Goose.

I followed the maze of shelves round and round until I came to the darkest corner and there, as I expected, I was blocked by the legs of the stepladder. Goose was quietly sitting on the platform at the top. She was crying. Knowing it was a completely stupid question but asking it anyway, I said, 'You OK, Goose?'

Goose shook her head, wiped her nose on the sleeve of her cardigan and sniffed.

Knowing the answer but asking anyway, I said, 'What's up?'

Wordlessly Goose reached down and handed me her phone. I took it and pressed a key, making the face light up.

There, on the screen, I read:

NEIL ADAM

going out wiv emily
now hope we can
still B friends
Sorry neil ☺

OPTIONS   BACK

It was a very horrible situation to be in. I puffed out my cheeks and then I said, 'Oh my God, Goose. You've been binned by text!'

I don't think it was the right thing to say. Goose just curled up tighter on the platform of the stepladder and started to cry all over again. I chewed my thumbnail and gawped helplessly at her. The thing is, with her sat high up there, it was very hard for me to do anything else. The best I could manage was a pointless pat on her ankle, which was just within reach. She was wearing those ESMERELDA daisy shoes.

And then Emily appeared and said, 'Um, there's a man waiting for a DWAYNE training shoe in size ten.'

This wasn't a good thing to say either. Goose lifted her head up and screeched, 'YOU STOLE MY MAN!' And then Emily started crying as well and then, just when the situation was getting really emotionally unstable, Dionne appeared from out of her office and said, 'Will somebody please tell me what's going on?'

Goose and Emily were too hysterical to speak so it was

left to ME to try to explain, but Dionne kept telling me to slow down a bit but I couldn't slow down a bit because I had loads to say, and then Dionne just sighed and told Goose to take the rest of the day off and Emily to go and wash her face, which was all smudged with mascara and red lipstick, and after that Gina was drafted in for the afternoon shift and she made me go through the whole sordid story again and I did and Gina didn't tell me to slow down because she's obviously quicker at listening than Dionne and then, when I'd finished, Gina said, 'Love. It causes nofink but an 'eadache. Oo needs it, Lottie? Oo needs it?'

And just for once I agreed with her.

Love and poetry, I reckon we could all do without them. And that's all I've got to say on the matter. Although I appreciate that this actually hasn't been as brief a word as I was expecting.

sOmetimes, i'D fOrGet mY heaD . . .

My mum has stolen my computer. She has taken it out of my bedroom and locked it in the loft. I am now forced to use the communal facilities in the school library, which is OK, but half of the computers at school are so slow I can feel myself physically ageing while the processor is whirring, and the other half have got sticky keyboards. If I catch bird flu or mange or anything else nasty from one of those sticky keyboards, it will be my mum's fault.

The problem started when I got up for school yesterday morning. I'd been so totally buzzing with stuff to say in this English coursework – about love and poetry, as you know – that I'd spent almost all of Saturday night and Sunday night thinking about things and then typing them up. In fact, I was so absorbed in intellectual pursuits that it was quite a while before I started to actually feel sleepy, and when I looked at the clock it was 4.17 a.m.

This gave me quite a shock. It is amazing just how quickly time can move when you are genuinely interested in something and how totally brain-meltingly slowly it can go in Mr Thomas's double-science lessons.

Anyway, I went to bed immediately then, because my first lesson of the week is always art with Mr Spanton and I never want to be late for that. Art is my most wicked and favourite subject ever. I climbed into bed and shut my eyes and got all warm and snugly, but I'd hardly been asleep for more than two microseconds when my alarm went off again and it said 7.00 a.m.

At first I thought it must be a digital malfunction. I picked up my clock and held it close to my eyes and checked again. It definitely said 7.00 a.m. I leaned over to the window which is right next to my bed, opened it a fraction and dropped my alarm clock out.

I dragged myself out of bed and off to the bathroom, thinking that perhaps a shower would make me feel better. It didn't. In fact, I don't know if it was because I had the water too hot or something, but when I came out of the shower and wrapped myself up in my towel, I went a bit dizzy and had to sit down on the cold tiles for a few minutes.

By the time I'd put on my school uniform and gone down to breakfast, I was feeling like this.

My mum was in the kitchen eating toast. When I walked in, she stood up, gave me a big massive hug and said, 'Happy birthday, sweetheart!'

I was so gobsmacked I think I stopped breathing. And then, fortunately, I started again and said, 'Is it really my birthday today?'

This time my mum looked gobsmacked. She gave me a funny look and said, 'Lottie, it's your fifteenth birthday. How on earth could you forget that?'

I couldn't think of any answer.

And then she said, 'Honestly, Lottie! You'd forget your head if it wasn't bolted on to your shoulders.'

My mum is always saying this to me. I don't like it. It makes me sound like I've got no neck.

My face went all hot and prickly and I got that dizzy feeling again that I'd had in the bathroom. My mum was still looking at me as if I was a mutant. I knew I needed to say something to make her chill out a bit so I shrugged my shoulders and said, 'So what? It's just a poxy birthday.'

My mum frowned and picked up a parcel that had been sitting on the worktop. It was all wrapped up in shiny purple paper with a silver ribbon. She held it in front of her and said, 'So you won't be wanting this then?'

I smiled at that point. Even when you're feeling like Doctor Death it's hard not to smile when being offered something wrapped up in shiny purple paper with a big silver ribbon.

'Thanks.' I tore off the paper while my mum watched. Inside was a box set of DVDs. I didn't recognize the film titles printed on the front. Feeling just a bit colossally confused, I read the titles out loud to myself.

'*East of Eden. Rebel Without a Cause. Giant.*'

The pictures on the box showed stills from ancient black-and-white films. I looked up at my mum. I was starting to feel a bit disappointed. I'd have preferred a Nintendog.

'Why have you given me a load of boring old films?'

I knew the moment I said it, that this was not a good

thing to say. If I could have rewound a few seconds and not said it, believe me, I would have done. But I couldn't.

My mum went all pink and said in a voice which had a really blatantly dangerous edge to it, '*James Dean*, Lottie! They're the films that James Dean made before he died!' And then, before I could apologize or anything, she said, 'You could at least *pretend* to be pleased. You know what? You can be terribly rude, sometimes, Charlotte, you honestly can!'

I hate it when she calls me Charlotte. She only ever calls me Charlotte when she's freaking out on me. And I'm not that wildly ecstatic about being called *rude* either. It affects my frame of mind in a very negative way. It makes me feel a bit edgy. Like this.

I said, 'Yeah, I like James Dean in *posters* but you know I can't deal with watching rubbishy old films. I *hate* old films. Old films bore me to death. The only old film I've ever sat all the way through is that stupid film about two gays sitting on a bench and that was well pathetic. What was it called again? *Forrest Gump*? Yeah, that's it. *Forrest Gump*. Well old – well pathetic.'

My mum took a deep breath and her eyes went very very narrow. I think she was starting to feel a bit edgy too.

She said, 'I thought you'd be pleased. I thought those posters meant you were a big James Dean fan. If *you* can't make your mind up about what you like and don't like, there's no hope for me, is there?'

She was genuinely upset. I could see that her eyes had gone watery. I felt EVEN worse then, but my mouth must have been hijacked by the devil because instead of trying to say anything remotely nice, I just said, 'Can I go now, please? I'm going to be late for art.'

My mum put her hand over her mouth as if she was trying to stop some bad words escaping from it. I thought that would be a good moment to leave. I'd got as far as putting my hand on the kitchen door when Mum said, 'Charlotte!'

I froze.

'For your information, Charlotte, *Forrest Gump* is not such an old film and it doesn't even have any gay people in it. And I don't want to hear you referring to gay people as *gays* again. It's not nice and it doesn't make *you* sound nice.'

I turned around. '*Gay?* It's a word. Everybody says it. *You* just said it.'

My mum stood up and put her head on one side in the way that she does whenever she's about to get a bit deep. 'There's a very big difference between referring to someone as *a gay person* and *a gay sitting on a bench*. You wouldn't like it if someone called you *a gay* or *a straight,* would you?'

'No, because I'm not a gay,' I said. I was nearly crying.

'No,' said my mum, 'and you're not just *a straight* either. You're a person, Lottie. You're you.'

I said, 'I thought you were in the normal police not the word police,' and then I picked up my Donna Karan shoulder bag and walked out of the kitchen, slamming the door as I went.

Breakfast in my house is not always like this.

aND theN it GOt wOrse

After that I didn't have a very good day. I ran all the way to school, only to discover that art had been cancelled. Instead of perfecting my forgery of *The Scream*,[12] I was ordered to sit in freezing silence in the sports hall and fill in one of those completely pointless and random questionnaires that we get forced to fill in from time to time. Somewhere, somebody is putting together a dossier of colossally useless bits of information on every pupil in Wales, perhaps even the world. The first question said:

Are you . . . ?

12-13 years old	14-15 years old	16-17 years old

Please tick.

I looked at it for ages. Around me, everyone else had their head down and was busy ticking boxes and turning pages. I just sat there thinking about James Dean on my bedroom wall. I used to be really into him once. I don't know why because he's only a sad, dead film star with sticky-up hair.

---

12 See footnote 9.

Then I thought about my mum and started to feel really bad and really guilty. It wasn't her fault that she'd bought me the world's most boring DVD box set. At least she'd actually remembered it was my birthday. Unlike me, apparently.

I looked down at the questionnaire again and frowned and then I finally put up my hand. Mrs Rowlands came over. She hates me.

'I don't know where to put my tick,' I whispered.

Mrs Rowlands looked down at the paper and then said, 'Haven't you even started the proper questions yet? What have you been doing all this time?'

'I've been wondering where to put my tick,' I whispered back.

Mrs Rowlands gave me a funny look and then said, 'Well, you know how old you are, don't you?'

'I'm fifteen,' I whispered. 'Today.'

'Well tick the box that says fourteen to fifteen.' She gave me another blatantly weird look and then started to walk away in the direction of Gareth Stingecombe, who also had his hand up.

'I can't,' I said to the back of Mrs Rowlands. 'I can't tick fourteen to fifteen because that's not how old I am.'

Mrs Rowlands spun round on her kitten heels and said, 'Sssshhhh! Whisper, please, Lottie! These are test conditions. What are you fussing about now?'

'I can't tick that box because it says tick here if your age is fourteen to fifteen years old, and my age isn't fourteen to fifteen years old. I'm fifteen today, which means that, technically, I'm *past* fifteen but I'm not yet between sixteen and seventeen, so there isn't a suitable category for me. If there was a category which said fifteen to sixteen I'd tick that one, but there isn't, so where do I put my tick because I'm not going to say I'm fourteen to fifteen years old when it blatantly isn't true.'

All this came out of my mouth very quickly. Somewhere along the way I'd also forgotten to whisper. Mrs Rowlands was looking a bit annoyed.

'SSSSSHHHH!' She gave me a dirty look and then said, 'Just tick the box that says fifteen in it.'

For the zillionth time that morning I felt my face go hot. All around me in the sports hall people were sitting still and filling in their questionnaires, but I couldn't fill in mine because there wasn't a category for me to fit into and it made me feel all agitated and anxious. I picked up my pencil and started tapping it on the desk.

'SSSSSSSSSHHHHHH!!!!' Mrs Rowlands gave me an '*I hate you Lottie Biggs*' look and then said, 'Stop being silly and just fill the thing in.'

And then I flipped. I stood up in the silent sports hall and said in a voice that was very loud:

'So you want me to tell lies now, is it? You want me to tell the nosy person who reads this that I'm actually younger than

I am. It's not *every* day you have a fifteenth birthday, you know. But for all you and this stupid questionnaire care, I'm actually living in some random twilight zone which doesn't even have its own bloody category. Well, it's NOT BLOODY funny living in a timeless black hole, actually. Not funny at all!'

I think I would have said more but by this time Mrs Rowlands had taken hold of me by the elbow and was half pulling, half pushing me out of the room. As I walked past the desk where Goose was sitting, I saw that she had stopped writing and was looking at me with a very worried expression on her face. I wanted to smile at her, but I was so wound up I think I'd forgotten how to. Then I walked past Gareth Stingecombe's desk and he had also put down his pencil and was looking rather worried. I tried to smile at him too, but my facial muscles weren't having any of it so instead, I just said, 'OH,

FOR GOD'S SAKE! NOT MORE BLOODY VIRGINS!'
Gareth went all purple and quickly put his head down. Then
I noticed that nearly every other person in the sports hall had
stopped writing and was looking at me. But most of these
others weren't looking worried – they were laughing.

For the rest of the day I was internally excluded. This
meant that I had to sit outside the head teacher's office
and read a book. By some weird twist of fate, the book I
was given was called *The Collected Poems of Stevie Smith*.
I sat and read the whole thing and then I sat and read it
through four times more. I still didn't understand any
of it.

When the bell eventually rang to signal the end of the
last lesson Goose came to find me. She was out of breath
because she'd run all the way from the science block
to catch me before I left. Seeing her cheered me up no
end.

I said, 'Goosey! How glad am I to see you! I've had to sit
here all day and read this boring book of poetry by that Stevie
Smith woman. I'm surprised I haven't dropped down dead
with terminal tedium. At one point I even thought about
asking if I could go to Mr Thomas and get some worksheets
on amoebas or something but there wasn't anyone around to
ask, so instead I just—'

'Happy Birthday, Lottie!' said Goose.

'. . . sat here reading this random poetry about people
called Croft who sit in lofts. I've read it all *five* flaming times

but it still doesn't make any sense to me. I reckon this Stevie Smith woman must have been totally off her flaming head or something. Her poems are—'

'Lottie, shut up a minute,' said Goose. 'I'm trying to wish you happy birthday.'

'Oh.' I stopped talking and felt a bit baffled. Then I remembered about my birthday and started laughing. It was really shaping up as the crappest birthday ever. Sometimes there's nothing else you can do other than laugh.

'I've got you a present,' said Goose. 'You want to go to the Dragon Coffee House and open it?'

This was definitely without a doubt the very best offer I'd had all day. We walked out of school and down past the graveyard. On the other side of the road, Elvis Presley was lying on his back on his public bench and bellowing, 'Are You Lonesome Tonight?' When he saw us walk by, he stopped and shouted, 'Hello shoe-shop girls,' and then he carried on singing. We shouted 'Hello' back.

I said to Goose, 'Do you reckon Elvis is a schizo or something?'

Goose frowned. 'I don't know, Lotts. I think he's harmless though.'

We walked on a bit further and then Goose said, 'I don't reckon we should call him a *schizo* though.'

'Why not? *Schizo* – it's a word. Everybody says it. What's wrong with that?'

Goose frowned. 'I don't think *everybody* says it. I don't think a doctor would actually refer to someone as a *schizo*. I can't imagine teachers saying it either. Or your mum. It just sounds a bit nasty.'

'All right, keep your wig on,' I said.

But when we reached the Dragon Coffee House, Neil Adam was sitting at a table with Emily. Goose saw them first. She went a bit pale for a second and then she shrugged bravely and said, 'I'm SO over it. Being kissed by him was like having my face sucked off by a jellyfish. She's welcome to him. Let's sit here by the window.'

We ordered double choco-mochaccinos (with extra cream and marshmallows) in big chunky mugs, and Goose gave me her presents. There were two of them. The first was a CD called *Destiny of Death* by Goose McKenzie and the Tribe of Pixies. I was well impressed. It almost looked like something you could buy in a shop. Goose smiled proudly and said, 'I produced it myself. And designed the CD cover. We've moved on from folk music and developed into a heavier gothic sound.'

I looked at Goose. Even though she's sometimes got mad hair, she doesn't look at all weird or scary enough to be the lead singer in a goth band. She's very pretty for a start, and in my opinion goths tend to veer towards uglydom. But then again, I suppose even Marilyn Manson must have looked fairly OK once. I smiled and said, 'Thanks, Goose, that's so cool,' and squeezed *Destiny of Death* into my authentic Donna Karan shoulder bag before moving on to the second present. Unwrapping it, I found that it was an unofficial James Dean calendar. I gave it a hard stare and then I put it down on the table.

'What's the matter?' asked Goose, reddening. 'I know we're halfway through the year already, but the pictures are nice.'

'Mmm. Thanks.' It was hard to force any excitement into my voice. I took a sip of my double choco-mochaccino. It wasn't the fact that Goose had bought me a knock-down bargain-bucket calendar that was bothering me. It was that it was a *James Dean* calendar. It reminded me of the box of DVDs my mum had given me, and thinking about my mum made me feel colossally bad all over again.

Goose said, 'Are you sure everything is OK, Lotts? It's just that, well, if you don't mind me saying, you've been acting very seriously weird recently.'

I stared into my drink. It was dark brown and frothy and housed in a mug which was bottle green and had a red dragon printed on the side. The mug was the same design as the aprons the staff were wearing. My mug had an ever-so-small chip on the rim. I looked at Goose's mug. Goose's mug was perfect.

I couldn't think of anything to say so I said nothing.

We sat there in silence for a bit and then Goose said, 'How's the English coursework going?'

The mention of my English project perked me up. I leaned forward in my seat and said, 'It's going really well, Goose. I've spent about eighteen hours on it and written about twenty-four thousand words.'

Goose's eyes grew to the size of dinner plates. She went very white, opened her mouth for a second, then closed it, and then opened it again and said, 'Oh shit! Did Woody really want us to write that much?'

I shrugged. 'I don't know, Goose, but when your head is buzzing with ideas, you just have to go with the creative flow, don't you?'

Goose fiddled with her mug for a moment or two and then said, 'Um, you know what? I should probably be going home now. I reckon I need to spend a bit of time on my coursework.' And then she got up and grabbed her bag and rushed off without even waiting for me. Goose can be totally weird sometimes.

aND theN MY Mum PiNCheD mY COmPuter

When I got home, my mum was actually in before me for once. She opened the front door, showed me a big chocolate cake which she was balancing on her other arm and said, 'Can we start your birthday again?'

I was so relieved I nearly burst into tears right there on the doorstep. After the day I'd had, I don't think I could have hacked coming home to another Situation Critical Red Alert. It was nice to have a bit of peace. It's just a shame it didn't last.

Mum gave me a kiss. 'Get your coat off and come and have a cup of tea. There are some cards through here which you need to open.'

Feeling a billion times happier than I had done all day, I hung up my coat and followed my mum into the kitchen. On the table were a pile of cards and a package. I picked up the package and looked at it. It was from my sister, Ruthie. Smiling, I ripped at the end. I'm not the kind of person who prefers to leave the best bits until last. I prefer to go straight for the prize. That is probably why I always eat the pizza topping before I eat the base and also probably why I read the last page of any book before I start at the beginning. I'm a go-getting, forward-thinking kind of girl.

Inside the parcel Ruthie had sent me a card with a picture of an orang-utan on the front. This made me even happier because orang-utans are my most favourite animal ever. I like the way they are bright ginger and I especially like the way that their arms look like skinny bits of wispy fuzz but are actually dead, dead strong. *You* try hanging from a tree by your arms and see how long you last. They are very deceptive, those fuzzy arms. Inside the card Ruthie had written: *Saw this card and thought of you, fart face. Have a fab day, Ruthie xxx*. If you didn't happen to know that Ruthie was highly intelligent, there is no way you'd ever be able to guess it. I put my hand back inside the package and pulled out a T-shirt, which also had an orang-utan on the front. Highly chuffed, I pulled the T-shirt over my head and wore it on top of my school jumper.

'This is from your dad.' My mum handed me an envelope with a Wrexham postmark. I opened it. Inside the card my dad had written: *Happy Fourteenth Birthday, Lottie. Lots of love from Dad, Sally and Caradoc.* He'd put a cheque for fifty pounds inside. He did that last year too. I stared at the words written in the card for a while and then sort of smiled a bit and put it down.

My mum raised her eyebrows and then ruffled my hair and said, 'Are you going to open the rest of your cards?'

'Yeah, in a minute. I just want to take my bag and this calendar up to my room.'

I climbed the stairs to my bedroom, pushed open the door and sat down on my bed. I wasn't really bothered that my dad hadn't quite remembered how old I was. To be fair to him, it's not easy to remember stuff like that sometimes. Not when I live in Cardiff and he lives in Oompa-Loompa land. I can't actually ever remember his phone number. I have to keep it written down in my address book. I've filed it under B for Biggs and it's right next to Beca Bowen's phone number, and the truth is I don't use either of those numbers all that much.

I sat on my bed and did my best to empty my head of all the other stuff and tried to focus on what it feels like to be fifteen. You would think that being fifteen would feel fundamentally different to being fourteen. You'd think that being fifteen would feel more wise or more sexy or more sophisticated. I sat there for ages though and I couldn't feel anything. And then I started thinking about how fifteen is already halfway to thirty, which is ancient. And then I started thinking about how fifteen is a quarter of the way to being sixty, which is too brain-bogglingly old to even contemplate. And then I started thinking about Goose's CD, which was called *Destiny of Death* and, all of a sudden, I started feeling really really totally miserable. I looked at my wall and saw posters filled with the black-and-white face of James Dean, who was young and handsome and famous. But dead.

And then I noticed my computer was missing.

At the top of my voice, I screamed:

'Mum! What's happened to my computer?'

I was already halfway down the stairs before I'd got the question out of my mouth. My mum stood in the hallway wiping her hands on a teatowel. She said, 'Stop shouting, Lottie. Nothing has happened to your computer.'

'Where is it then?'

My mum looked a bit shifty and said, 'Come through to the kitchen, Lottie. I want to have a chat with you.'

I didn't like the sound of this. I could feel myself getting all aggravated. It felt all itchy, like nettlerash.

I followed my mum into the kitchen and sat down at the table. My foot was tap-tap-tapping against the chairleg.

My mum sat down next to me, rested her chin in her palm and looked me right in the eyes. 'What time did you go to bed last night?'

'What?' The question blatantly had nothing to do with where my computer was.

My mum said again, 'I want to know what time you went to bed and went to sleep.'

I frowned. 'I dunno. I was doing my English coursework.'

'Until when?'

'I dunno.' I shifted in my seat and started drumming my fingers on the table. As I've said before, I've never been the type of person who likes being put on the spot. I don't perform well under pressure.

My mum sighed. 'It's just that when you woke up this morning you were all over the place. You hadn't even remembered that it was your own birthday. And then when I got home from work today, there was a message from the school saying that you'd been removed from lessons all day because of disruptive behaviour. They're worried about you, Lottie. And so am I. I've heard this all before and I didn't like it then and I don't like it now. And if you remember, Doctor Crosby told us that it is very important that you get plenty of sleep each night if you want to stay fit and healthy.'

I stopped drumming my fingers on the table and put my head in my hands. I'd forgotten that the school would phone my mum. And I'd sort of forgotten about the time that my mum had forced me to see our family GP, Dr Crosby. It was during the summer holidays, last year, when I'd been feeling a bit weird in the head for some reason and stopped washing my hair. I didn't wash my hair for over a month, and then my mum took me to see Dr Crosby. He said it was probably due to my age and told my mum that I should eat plenty of vegetables and go to bed earlier. But then he told my mum that I also needed to speak to a counsellor. I think it was because *he* was getting bored of talking to me. He'd seen me before that, you see, about that time in Year 9 when Samantha Morgan drove me mad and made me get chucked out of school. Then I told my mum I wasn't going to see a counsellor because I'm not mental. I told my dad, and he got really angry with my mum and said that no child of his needed to see a shrink and that she was causing a great big fuss over nothing. Then he took me on holiday with him and Sally and Caradoc to Spain. Spain was OK but Sally didn't like the heat that much so I spent all of the first week left on the beach with Caradoc while she and dad sat in the hotel bar. The funny thing is, I don't really like blazing sunshine all that much myself. In the second week I put my foot down and told dad that I'd had enough of the beach so then he enrolled me and Caradoc into a kids' club. The club was only supposed to be for four- to twelve-year-olds but Dad paid a bit extra so they'd take me too. I told him I didn't want to go, but he just laughed and said it would do me good. Apart from a weird eleven-year-old boy who kept trying to hold my hand, everyone else was primary-school age. I only went to that tragic club twice, and then I went all weird with sunstroke or something and wouldn't get out of bed for the rest of the week.

Somehow I'd forgotten all about that holiday and Dr Crosby, even though it wasn't all that long ago. But my mum, it seems, never forgets anything. Feeling my aggravation rise, I shook my head and said, 'Honestly, Mum, it wasn't my fault. There wasn't a category for me to put my age into.'

'Lottie, it doesn't matter about that.' My mum was still looking me right in the eyes. 'I'm just concerned that you're not getting enough sleep. What on earth are you doing on that computer all night? You're not talking to people in chat rooms, are you?'

I rolled my eyes and gave a big noisy frustrated sigh. 'Oh honestly, Mum. I have got *real* friends, you know. I told you, I've been doing my English coursework, that's all. There's no law against that, is there?'

'No, there isn't, but I'm not having you sitting up all night doing it when you should be sleeping.'

'I haven't been feeling tired.'

My mum looked at me a little nastily and said, 'You've been *acting* tired.'

I started to feel desperate. The thing is, you see, I really need that computer. Without it, this entire English coursework project could go belly up. I said, 'So how exactly am I going to do my schoolwork?'

My mum said, 'You can use my laptop on the kitchen table in the evenings after tea.'

I opened my mouth to protest, but before I even had a chance to groan, my mum said, 'Don't worry, I've already saved all your files on to a disc for you. Aren't I wonderful?'

I didn't answer this. I couldn't because I was too furious to speak. My mum just carried right on talking anyway.

'And you can use the facilities at school. But until I can trust you not to stay awake all night and then go getting yourself into trouble with your teachers because you haven't had any sleep, *your* computer will stay locked in the loft. End of discussion.'

So now I'm reduced to using the scatty school facilities in homework club. Me. In homework club.

THE SHAME!!!

I haven't told Goose.

NOt sLeePiNG is NOt fuNNY

Since my mum stole my computer I have been totally and utterly unable to sleep. In fact, I would even go so far as to say that I am sleep deprived. This is a blatant example of irony. Today in school Mr Wood wasted seventeen minutes and twelve seconds trying to explain to our class what irony means. In the end I had to help him out. Mr Wood was going about it all wrong. He was confusing everyone by using intellectual examples from that play *Macbeth*, which nobody really understands anyway because it's written in the language of the ancient druids.

Mr Wood had his eyes shut and his glasses in his hand and was droning something that went along the lines of, 'When Macduff says *Look to the lady*, this is a moment of high dramatic irony because we – the audience – know that Lady Macbeth is a scheming, wicked, heartless charlatan. She is certainly not a lady.'

It's not Mr Wood's fault, but he happens to have a voice like a foghorn and sometimes it can be very difficult to stay interested in what he is saying.

At the back of the class Lee Fogel's hand shot up. 'But she *is* though, sir. That's why she's called *Lady* Macbeth.'

Mr Wood opened his eyes and frowned. 'I don't think you quite follow me, Lee. What I'm saying is that there is a *huge* disparity between our notion of what a lady should be and *her conduct*, and Macduff's usage of *lady* here seems misguided and ridiculous.'

Lee said, 'Huh?'

Everyone was shifting in their seats. Beca Bowen had got her nail file out. I was getting a bit bored and fed up so I put my hand up and said, 'I think what Mr Wood is trying to say is that irony is about weird contradictions. Macduff *thinks* that Lady Macbeth is a gentle, delicate, womanly woman, but actually she's a minging troll bitch from hell.'

A light of understanding came on somewhere behind Lee's eyes. I was on a roll so I continued, 'I mean, it's like what's happened to me since my mum stole my computer. She took it out of my bedroom because she thought I was working too late on it and not getting enough sleep. It is therefore deeply ironic that I have been unable to sleep one single wink since it left my room.'

I sat back and folded my arms. Mr Wood took off his glasses and frowned. Then he said, 'Yes, that example would work. Thank you, Charlotte.'

The thing is though, apart from being a premium example of irony, not being able to sleep is also a premium example of mental torture. It was Monday when my mum committed her act of thievery. It's now Friday and I don't think I've properly lost consciousness once. Not even for a second. I am starting to feel desperate. It was fine when I was sat up all night typing because then I wasn't thinking about sleeping, I was thinking about my coursework. But now I've got nothing to do except lie awake at night and think about trying to go to sleep. And I can't. If you want to know what that feels like, imagine that you're massively tired but every time you shut your eyes your feet start to tap-dance and Cardiff Airport opens up a new terminal inside your head.

It is the most hideous thing in the whole world EVER.

Part 2

a NOte fOr the eXamiNer

Dear Mr (or Mrs) Examiner

I know that to you I am nothing more than another piece of coursework in your massive pile of marking, but I'd just like to take this opportunity to remind you that I am an actual human person with actual human problems. And my life is a bit complicated at the moment. This means:

1. I haven't got access to a computer.

As you already know, my mum has confiscated mine, and I'm not in the mood to sit in the kitchen and borrow hers. I'd rather stay in my bedroom. So please excuse my handwriting.

2. As you can see, I am dividing my creative-writing project into two parts.

When I began writing this I did not intend this to happen. To be honest, I was only expecting it to be a couple of pages long. But the thing is, see, since I last sat down and wrote anything, my life has changed completely. Everything written before this point was written by a normal person. Everything from here onward has been written by a social menace. This could seriously affect the quality of whatever you are about to read. It is not easy to concentrate on coursework when you are officially under surveillance by the South Wales Police.

Please could you bear this in mind when you are deciding what grade to give me.

Thank you.

Lottie Biggs

a sCreaM DaY

Today, Saturday 21 June, has been a day of Shockingly Crappy Rubbish at Every Abysmal Moment (SCREAM). In fact, it has been a disaster. I have only previously had two such awful days in my entire life. The first was the SCREAM day we had six years ago when we discovered my dad had left us and was running away to Wrexham to live with Sally. That day had been rubbish from the offset. Ruthie had woken me up and said, 'Dad's gone. He's taken his CDs and everything. Mum says he's gone to live with Sally.' Sally worked in the same office as my dad. Ruthie and I had both met her a few times when we'd been ill and mum couldn't get a day off from fighting crime. I'd got to know Sally quite well because when I was seven I broke my leg and ended up being off school for practically an entire term. She'd always been really nice to me and often gave me sweets. I think it's fair to say that I liked her. I never wanted her to run away with my dad though.

Me and Ruthie didn't go to school that day and my mum didn't go to work. We all spent the whole day crying. In the evening my dad showed up looking tired and upset. He also had a trendy new haircut. My mum went upstairs while my dad told me and Ruthie how he still loved us but he also loved Sally and he needed to go and live with her. Ruthie got up then and called my dad a very rude word and stormed out of the room. I can remember exactly what she said very

very clearly, and I remember too that it made me start to cry all over again because I'd never heard Ruthie say bad stuff like that before and it was pretty shocking. After that it was ages before Ruthie spoke to him again. Literally MONTHS and MONTHS. Every time my dad rang us up Ruthie refused to come to the phone, and every time he visited she'd go upstairs and shut herself in her bedroom until he'd gone again. Then one day, just before she went off to university, Dad came round with a stack of archaeology books and a cake which said GOOD LUCK RUTHIE on it and the two of them finally went and had a long-overdue talk and now I think they get on fairly OK. The weird thing is that I can remember this stuff about Ruthie freaking out really clearly, but I can't actually remember that much about how I felt. I suppose it's not really something I like to mull over very much.

The other SCREAM day was just a couple of years ago on 24 December, when Cerys, my pet rabbit, died. She was a Netherland Dwarf with a whitish body and smoky-grey ears and feet. She also had a smoky-grey nose. I'd had her for more than EIGHT years, which is an epic age for a Netherland Dwarf rabbit. If she was a human person, she'd probably have had a birthday card from the Queen. I know that it might seem a bit wet to be emotionally devastated by the death of a rabbit, but I was really attached to Cerys and I am not ashamed to admit it. It is also a very nasty thing to have happened literally just before Christmas. This is a picture of what she looked like in her prime.

*

I had to lie on the grass for absolutely ages to get this photograph. Seeing it now makes me feel fractionally better. Cerys was a very happy and independent little rabbit, who used to live in a hutch  at the bottom of our garden. Even though she was little, she wasn't at all frightened of cats. If anything, they were more terrified of her because she could be surprisingly fierce when she wanted to be.

One day I did see her really scared though. I looked out of the window and she was standing on her back legs in the middle of the lawn with her ears all alert and a look of total panic all over her furry little face. I looked around the garden but I couldn't see anything and then, for some reason, I looked up into the air. Hanging really high in the sky was a great big kestrel, just flapping its wings and looking right down at my little Cerys and probably licking its lips.[13] I screamed and ran out into the garden, and Cerys broke out of her petrified panic and legged it for the bushes. The great big

---

[13] Do kestrels have lips?

kestrel hung there in the sky for a few more seconds and then it circled a couple of times before finally flying off. The moral of this story is that YOU NEVER KNOW WHAT DANGERS COULD BE LURKING OVER YOUR HEAD. One minute you could be lying in the sun, happily eating grass and twitching your little nose, and the next minute you could be attacked and eaten by a kestrel. Life mings.

And don't I know it.

Because today has been the most hideous day of them all. Even that poet woman Stevie Smith could not have experienced a day any worse than the one I've just had and she wrote a poem that starts:

> My life is vile
> I hate it so
> I'll wait awhile
> And then I'll go.

This poem is called 'The Reason'. It makes a lot more sense to me than any of her other poems. I sat on the floor of my bedroom and read this poem just a couple of hours ago and it had a very powerful effect on me. To begin with, it made me smile because its bluntness is kind of funny and it doesn't exactly seem like she killed herself trying too hard to write anything clever, and then I really started to laugh at the fact that such a rubbish and pointless poem could ever have been printed in a book for me to read. But then, as I was laughing, I noticed that my face was all wet and my nose was all slimy and I realized that I needed a box of tissues very urgently, and while I was wiping my eyes and blowing my nose I began to feel extremely desperately sad for Stevie, because when you think about what she is saying you soon realize that something REALLY AWFUL must have happened inside her head to make her say anything so tragically hopeless and then I started feeling extremely sad for myself as well. My mum heard me crying and knocked on the door and asked if she could come in, but I was so talked out by then that I told her I needed to be on my own for a bit, and my mum must have been all talked out as well because I heard her sigh heavily and go back downstairs. And I sat there all curled up on the floor of my bedroom feeling miserable for ages and then, finally, I picked up this project again and started writing some more.

Just like that other SCREAM day six years ago, today was also rubbish from the outset. I got up this morning when my mum banged on my door at 7.45. She's been banging on my door every morning this week because my alarm clock has weirdly disappeared out of my room. Don't think I've been having lovely lie-ins though because, as I've already explained, I blatantly cannot sleep. I am actually about as awake as the most awake person in the whole of Awake Land. That is how wide awake I am! But even so, I've been experiencing one or two problems getting out of bed. It just seems to involve more effort than I can be bothered to make.

'All right, all right, I'm getting up,' I shouted, and then under my breath I muttered, 'No need to get your knickers in a knot.'

I forced myself into a standing position and put on my dodgy skirt and blouse for work. In a way it was almost a relief to be doing something other than lying in bed going nuts. I still wasn't feeling good though. I had a really massive headache.

I couldn't be bothered to have a wash so I just went downstairs and ate a Pot Noodle and then left the house quickly before my mum could start moaning at me.

When I got to work I had my first nasty surprise of the day. Gina was in. She was standing at the till surrounded by rolls of YOU PAY stickers and black plimsolls. When she saw me, she said, 'Good of you to join us, Missy Biggs. You're late.'

I said, 'No, I'm not. I'm five minutes early.'

Gina gave me one of those smiles that doesn't involve anything friendly happening around the eyes and said, 'As Head Saturday Girl, you should really be here in plenty of time to help prepare the shop.'

'Prepare the shop for what?' I asked.

'For the day ahead,' said Gina, very loudly and very slowly as if I had hearing problems and learning difficulties. 'Customers want to walk into a bright vibrant shop with bright vibrant staff, and preparation is the key to good sales figures, young lady. To fail to prepare is to prepare to fail.'

I looked Gina right in the eye and said, 'Yeah, whatever,' and then I walked over to the door at the back of the shop so I could get away from her and hang my coat and bag up. Before I left the shop floor though I hesitated and said, 'Why are you in today, Gina, and what time are you off?'

Gina smiled just from the mouth again and said, 'Dionne's under the weather and I'll be in all day.'

'Terrific-horrific,' I muttered and shoved my backpack on to a hook before disappearing off to the furthest corner of the stockroom so that I could climb up the stepladder to sit and think.

I was still up the ladder when first Emily and then Goose arrived. I heard Gina tell them they were late and I heard Goose make up some story about her front door being jammed and then I heard the hoover being switched on. I didn't hear Goose and Emily speak to each other so I guessed that they were still not on speaking terms. After a while I heard the door to Dionne's office close and the muffled one-sided conversation of Gina on a telephone. Guessing it was safe to move, I went back out into the shop. Both Goose and Emily looked quite grateful to see me. It's not nice being confined within the same space as someone you'd rather not speak to. I should know because I have this experience whenever I'm in a classroom with Mrs Rowlands. I pulled some laces out of some shoes and then I stuck a few YOU PAY stickers on the wall and then I wasted some time spying on Keith Bright, who was wandering around his empty optician's and having a long conversation with somebody on his mobile phone. Every now and then he'd laugh and run the palm of his hand over his bouffant grey hair and check himself out in a mirror in the corner of his shop. I think he's got bored of me and Goose and is in love with somebody else. I must be the only person left in the entire world who doesn't know what love is. Except for Gina, obviously.

After a while of watching Keith, me and Goose went back out to the stockroom and sat on the ladders and had a chat. Goose told me that I needed to re-do my hair because my beige roots were showing, but I told her I couldn't be bothered. After all, what's the point of colouring your hair when you've got a face like a smashed potato? Then we pulled some shoeboxes off the shelf which were called CHARLOTTE ladies lace-ups in brown and Goose laughed a bit at how hideous the shoes inside were, and I tried to laugh but I was feeling so tired and terrible that nothing seemed very funny. Slowly the minutes ticked away until lunch. And all in all it would have been a very average and boring morning indeed had it not been for the danger which was lurking unseen over my head, just waiting for the right moment to swoop down and mess up my life.

as i was takiNG MY BaG Off the hOOk

Art is my favourite subject. English is my second and history
is my third. If it wasn't for the fact that my school is forcing
me to study the rise of Communism and the onset of the Cold
War, history would possibly be even higher on my list. The
thing I really like about history has nothing to do with dates of
wars or any of that stuff. Those are just random facts to
memorize pointlessly to impress examiners. What I really like
to think about is the impact that one second in one person's life
can have on the whole future of the world. Take King Harold I,
for example. Everyone knows that he got an eyeful of arrow
at the Battle of Hastings. But what if, while he was fighting his
battle against William (the Great Duke of Normandy), he'd
decided that second to look down and not up just as the
arrow flew through the air on course to take his eye out. If
he'd looked downwards, the arrow would have bounced off
his metal helmet and he wouldn't have been killed and the
battle would have continued. Maybe he'd then have fired
an arrow that killed William instead. Or maybe the Normans
would have eventually got fed up with fighting and decided
to go back home to France. Harold would have remained as
King of England. The English language wouldn't be full of French
words, and Wales wouldn't be full of Norman castles. Maybe,
without the castles, the Welsh would have grown stronger and
stronger and driven out the English. Maybe the Welsh would
have invaded England and everybody round the world would be

speaking Welsh today. Just think! Rugby would be the biggest sport in the world. Shirley Bassey would be the queen. Cardiff would be the biggest city in Great Britain. All this is PERFECTLY POSSIBLE if Harold had just looked down and not got an arrow in the eye. But he looked up.

And as I was taking my bag off the hook to go for my lunch I looked down when I should have looked up. One second would have changed everything. I would have looked up just in time to see that a pile of shoeboxes filled with CHARLOTTE ladies lace-ups in brown were in the process of toppling forward and were now on a fast-moving crash-collision course with the top of my head. And then I would have made a quick darting move to the left or right and I would have been spared the hideous trauma which followed. But I didn't look up.

As I was taking my bag off the hook, nine boxes of CHARLOTTE ladies lace-ups in brown finally lost their battle against gravity and came raining down on me. My hands flew upwards to protect my head, and my backpack, full to bursting point with shoes I can't even remember rescuing, fell to the floor and spilled open. And at just that same moment, Gina walked in.

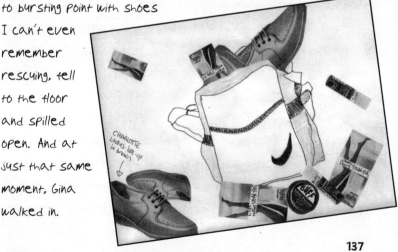

CHARLOTTE
ladies lace-up
in brown

aND theN i GOt stuCk DOwN a MeNtaL MaNhOLe

Gina looked down at me as I squatted on the floor with my head in my hands. And then, without saying a word, she stooped over, picked up my bag and looked inside it. Slowly I stood up. The nine boxes of CHARLOTTE ladies lace-ups in brown hadn't really hurt me, but my head was banging from the inside as if my brain was trying to burst its way out. I suddenly felt very wobbly and very panicky. For no reason at all, I did the worst thing possible. I started to laugh. A few little squeaks escaped nervously from the side of my mouth and then, just as if there was a whole army of amoebas tickling my insides with feathers, I opened my mouth and started to howl with laughter. Seriously howl. I was rocking. Tears were streaming down my face and I was laughing so hard that I could barely breathe.

Gina said, 'Do you think this is funny?'

Something about this question made the amoebas inside me shift up a gear and start tickling me even harder. I gave a massive snort and laughed so hard that my body collapsed inwards at the waist and I was temporarily incapable of standing up straight.

Gina said, 'Your bag contains a pair of Sole Mates shoes and . . .' she broke off to look back down at my offending backpack which was still in her hands ♥ five pairs of Sole Mates tights. I'm also well aware of the three cans of

138

Leather Shine that rolled across the floor as I came in. And the two cans of foot-odour spray. Were you planning to pay for any of these?'

I breathed in and out slowly and concentrated hard on not laughing.

Gina said again, 'Were you planning to pay for any of these?'

I don't like being put on the spot. I am not a person who answers well when placed under pressure.

Gina said for a third time, and there was by now a definite hint of something nasty in her voice, 'Were you planning to pay for any of these?'

I looked down at the stuff on the floor and then I looked at my bag, which was still in Gina's hands, and a big heavy lump of confusion hit me on the head. I wasn't really sure what I'd been planning to do with it all. I couldn't actually even remember taking any of it.

I slowly puffed out my cheeks. 'I don't know.'

Gina's voice grew a little nastier still. 'Just lately, our stock levels don't seem to be tallying with the records. Have you been helping yourself to other things?'

I frowned and tried to think back to the previous Saturday, but my head was still thumping and banging and the strain of thinking too hard was starting to make me feel really sick and dizzy. It had gone completely black inside my head. The air felt hot and stuffy and I realized for the first time ever that there wasn't a single window in the stockroom. All of a sudden, I felt really panicky. It was just as if I'd fallen down a deep manhole that had been left uncovered in the street.

I said, 'I don't know.'

Gina narrowed her eyes till I couldn't look at her any more. I looked down at my feet. I was wearing LAYLA ballet pumps in size four. Even now, I have no idea whether I ever paid for them or not.

Gina said, 'Come with me, young lady.' Still firmly grasping my bag, she turned and opened the door to the office, pausing for me to enter ahead of her. My feet did as they were told. The rest of me was feeling lousy.

'Sit down,' she said.

I did.

Gina crossed over to the desk, picked up the phone and punched some numbers into the keypad. I sat on the chair and stared helplessly at my LAYLA ballet pumps. I don't know why I was wearing them; I've never liked them. After a moment Gina

LAYLA
ballet pump
↓

said, 'Hello . . . Yes . . . It's Gina Jones from Sole Mates shoe shop, Whitchurch. One of my Saturday girls has been caught stealing from us . . . Charlotte Biggs . . . Yes . . . Yes. That would be helpful. Yes . . . Ok, thank you.'

Gina put down the phone and said, 'You just sit there and think about what you're going to say. The police are on their way to pick you up.'

aLOft iN the LOft

My mum works for South Wales Police in the Crime Investigations Department. She is based in a big concrete building right in the middle of the city centre. I've often seen this building on the news when reporters speak from the steps outside and wait for glimpses of criminals in orange boiler suits as they are bundled into the backs of big black vans. My mum has been a police officer for as long as I can remember. In fifteen years and five days I never once got to visit her place of work. On the first Saturday — the sixth day — of my fifteenth year, I am sorry to say that this situation has changed.

The corridor was dimly lit and smelt of something nasty. It wasn't vomit or wee or anything obviously horrific; it was a smell that was harder to put your finger on. Like the inside of a boy's boot bag. Or the bottom of a hamster's cage. Screwed on the wall, just to the left of my head, was a huge metal sign which said:

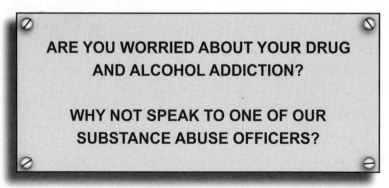

ARE YOU WORRIED ABOUT YOUR DRUG AND ALCOHOL ADDICTION?

WHY NOT SPEAK TO ONE OF OUR SUBSTANCE ABUSE OFFICERS?

Underneath this sign, with a red marker pen, somebody had written:

YOUR NUM IS A MAN

Underneath that, with a black pen, somebody else had written:

she's still
more sexy than You!

On a wooden bench, bolted into a recess in the wall, I sat, rocking. I'd been rocking, ever so slightly at first, for over an hour. Now I was starting to rock fairly hard. I'd built up quite a momentum, which began in my thighs and continued up the small of my back as I propelled my upper body backwards and forwards with increasing energy. Somewhere along the way I'd slipped into a faultless rhythm accompanied by the sound of a fast-paced creak of the bench as I rocked forwards and a dull thud from my back as I rocked backwards against the wall.

It went like this:

CREAK–THUD
CREAK–THUD
CREAK–THUD
CREAK–THUD
CREAK–THUD
CREAK–THUD
CREAK–THUD
CREAK–THUD
CREAK–THUD

It was nearly loud enough to cover the muffled and distant sound of the scary man who was shouting and swearing at the top of his voice from behind one of the mustard-yellow metal doors lining my corridor. But not quite. Not quite loud enough for that.

Opposite my Recess of Shame was an office which was

surrounded by big glass windows and brightly illuminated from within. Inside it was a policeman with grey hair and a grumpy face. He had spoken to me once when I'd arrived. He now opened up a little window inside his big window and said, 'Can't you sit still?'

I completely froze for a few minutes and then, when I was sure he was no longer looking at me, I started rocking again.

I don't know how long I sat there rocking. It must have been quite some time though because my belly had started to growl really loudly and I remembered that I'd never actually got to have my lunch; in fact, the only thing I'd eaten all day was a Pot Noodle at half past eight in the morning, and Pot Noodles don't exactly fill you up for very long. But still I sat there rocking and this time I could hear:

CREAK–THUD
GROWWWWLLLL
CREAK–THUD
GROWWWWLLLL

And I probably would have just sat there forever, listening to the rhythm of my rocking and listening to my belly grumble and trying not to listen to the bad language which was being shouted by the scary man from behind one of the metal doors, had I not started to need the toilet.

For a while, I just carried on rocking because I didn't know what else to do and, to be honest, I wasn't exactly sure any more if I could stop even if I wanted to. But pretty soon, the need to wee began to make my stomach hurt and I stood up. The grumpy old policeman shot up and opened his window again.

'Where do you think you're off to?'

'I need the toilet,' I said.

I watched as the GOP took a key from a hook on the wall of his office and attached it to a huge chain on his belt. Then he opened a side-door and signalled for me to follow him.

The GOP stopped outside one of the mustard-yellow metal doors and unlocked it with his key.

'This one's empty,' he said. 'You can use the loo in here. I'll wait outside, if you don't mind.'

I walked through the door. Inside was a small room with no windows. On one wall was a low bench with a blue plastic mattress on it. On the other wall was another metal sign about drugs and alcohol. In the corner of the room, squashed in between the near wall and the end of the blue mattress, was a metal toilet. It had no lid and no seat and there was no sign of any toilet paper. I looked at it long and hard and then I opened up the mustard-yellow metal door again.

'That was quick!' said the GOP.

146

'Am I supposed to use that thing?' I said, and pointed at the metal toilet.

'Well, what else do you think it is?' said the GOP. 'A dentist's chair?' He was clearly a very funny guy, this grumpy old policeman. Not!!

'I'm not using that.'

The GOP laughed but it wasn't a very nice laugh. 'That's the best I can offer you. Think yourself lucky. Some of the cells have only got a bucket.' And then he folded his arms and looked at his watch as if he had a plane to catch.

I looked back at the toilet. I was starting to feel desperate. But obviously not that desperate. From the next room the scary man began to shout and swear again, making me jump.

'How long do I have to be here?' I asked the GOP. And then before he could answer I added, 'What's happening to me?'

'Are you going to use the loo or not?'

I looked back into the cell and shook my head.

The GOP made an irritated noise and led me back up the corridor towards my Recess of Shame. As we passed one of the mustard metal doors a great commotion erupted from inside and the man who had been shouting and swearing since my arrival screamed out, 'Let me out of here, you bastards, or I'll piss on the floor.'

The grumpy old policeman gave a deep sigh and muttered, 'That'll help!' Then he jerked his head at the bench in the recess and said, 'Now sit down.'

I sat down. The GOP stood in the corridor, looking at me, with his arms folded over his fat stomach.

'The reason you've got to wait here is because we can't interview you without a supporting adult present. That would usually be a parent. And at the moment we're having some problems getting hold of one—'

'If my mum's not working, she usually goes out shopping on a Saturday,' I interrupted.

The GOP carried on talking as if I hadn't said anything. '☙ and unless we can get hold of one, we'll have to get a social worker in. And depending on whether or not any social workers are available, that could take thirty minutes or it could take several hours. So you're just going to have to sit quiet and be patient and hope that somebody at home gets our telephone messages pretty sharpish.'

I bit my lip. Then I leaned forward and put my head in my hands.

The GOP said, 'Bit late crying about it now, young lady. You should have thought about that when you were helping yourself to things that don't belong to you.'

I sat up, swallowed hard, took a deep breath and said, 'My mum does have a work phone which is always on. I don't know what the number is off by heart but you'd be able to find out easy enough.'

The GOP looked at me for a moment. He had a very stern face. He reminded me a bit of my Welsh teacher, Mrs Rowlands, except that he was blatantly a man of course.

'Where does your mother work?' he asked.

I put my hand over my mouth to stop myself from being sick and then, ever so quietly, I said, 'Here.'

'Pardon?' said the GOP.

'Here,' I whispered.

'Take your hand away from your mouth and then maybe I'll be able to hear you.'

I did as I was told, took another deep, deep breath and almost shouted,

'Here.'

At this, the grumpy old policeman almost smiled. He leaned back against the mustard door behind him. 'Well, well, well. And what is your mother's name?'

I stared at the writing on the wall next to me.

YOUR MUM IS A MAN

In my mind's eye I could see myself taking out a marker pen and writing underneath:

MY MUM IS GOING TO GO FLIPPING MENTAL

'Detective Sergeant Carolyn Biggs,' I said.

'Detective Sergeant Carolyn Biggs,' repeated the GOP, and then he said again, 'Well, well, well.' And then he left.

I sat right back on the wooden bench and leaned against the wall. The pain in my stomach had disappeared. It was almost as if my body had given up wanting the toilet and forgotten about it. Down the corridor I could still hear the scary madman ranting and raving. It wasn't a nice place that my mum worked in and I was glad she'd never brought me here. I closed my eyes and tried to think about something different, something which would calm me down and stop me thinking about what was going to go through my mum's head when her phone beeped and ruined her day off. And about what she'd say when she heard that her younger daughter had been arrested. And the weird thing is that all I could think of was Stevie Smith and that crazy poem of hers which goes 'Alott, in the lott, sits Crotti he is sott.' Except that in my head, I'd changed the words so that it now went:

> Alott,
> In the lott,
> Sits Lottie;
> She is potty.

And I kept saying it over and over and over to myself until my mum came.

*

The next room I saw was not much bigger than the cell with the toilet in and almost as grim. There were no windows in there either. Inside, there was nothing except a table and four chairs. On the table was a big old-fashioned tape recorder. On the chairs were me and my mum and two policemen: a man and a woman. My mum had surprised me. When the grumpy old policeman had opened up his little window to tell me that my mum had arrived and I could now be interviewed, I thought that I was about to be at the centre of a murder scene. I thought that she was going to go completely stark raving mental. But she hadn't at all. She'd just looked at me with a face that was all lined with sadness and worry and silently shaken her head. For the first time in my life I noticed that she was starting to look a little bit old. I felt awful then. I felt like it was my badness that had put those lines on her face. This feeling was worse than getting shouted at.

The man policeman said, 'My name is Detective Sergeant Giles and this —' he nodded at the woman — 'is Detective Constable Arbon. I need to ask a few routine questions and then, when we've got those out of the way, you'll be interviewed with the tape on. Do you understand?'

I nodded. Detective Sergeant Giles was tall and thin with black hair. He had a nice face and a kind voice and made me feel ever so fractionally better. But only by about one-eightieth. His colleague, Detective Constable Arbon, was short and fat with blonde hair. She didn't have a nice face and she hadn't spoken a single word since I'd entered the room but was eyeing me with a clear and blatant look of disapproval.

I didn't like her at all. I leaned forward, cupped my chin in my hands and sneaked a look at her identity card. It had DC Ellen Arbon written on it.

'Can you just confirm that your full name is Charlotte Beryl Biggs?'

DS Giles placed a clipboard on the table and patted his pockets for a pen. He found one and tucked it behind his ear, and then, from somewhere beneath him, he produced a greasy paper bag, which he set down on the table next to the clipboard.

My mum nudged me and hissed, 'Pay attention, Lottie, and answer the question.'

'Yes,' I said. 'But I've binned the Beryl bit and prefer to call myself just Lottie.'

DS Giles smiled ever so ever so slightly and said, 'And can you just confirm your address, please Charlotte.'

I sighed. 'Sixty-two, Springfield Place, Whitchurch.'

'And your date of birth?'

While he was speaking to me, DS Giles had taken a large pork pie and a sachet of tomato sauce out of the paper bag. He pulled the pastry lid off the top of his pie, squirted red sauce all over the pork inside and then pressed the lid back on. Then he picked the whole thing up and took a large bite. I watched him, fascinated. Though it made me feel a bit sick, to be honest.

My mum gave me another nudge. I jumped in my seat and quickly answered his question before my mum could poke me again. With one hand DS Giles ate his pie, and with the other he wrote something down on a form which was attached to his clipboard.

'Ok,' he said when he'd finished his pie. 'We're going to start the interview now. DC Arbon will say a few details out loud for the tape, and then you just answer the questions as best you can.'

I don't mind admitting that by now my head was starting to swim. I still hadn't eaten anything since the Pot Noodle way back at half past eight in the morning, and I couldn't even remember the last time I'd visited the toilet. DC Arbon had leaned forward and pressed down the play and record buttons on the tape recorder and was saying a whole bunch of boring stuff out loud, like what my name was and what day it was and what I'd done wrong, and my mum was still just sitting there quietly next to me, not going mental and looking a bit old.

DS Giles said, 'Did you put the shoes and the polish and the foot-odour spray in your bag, Charlotte?'

I nodded my head. DC Arbon said, 'Can you speak up for the tape?'

'Yes,' I said.

'And did you intend to pay for them?'

I thought about this question for a moment and then I said exactly the same as I'd said to Gina and it was the truth. 'I don't know.'

DS Giles said, 'Well, put it this way, Charlotte — would you have paid for those items today if they hadn't been found in your bag?'

And I didn't know how to answer that so I started biting my fingernails and tried to think of something helpful to say, but the only thing I could think about was how DS Ellen Arbon's name backwards was NO BRA NELLE and that wasn't exactly very helpful at all because all it did was make me laugh.

My mum took hold of my arm and shook it and almost shouted, 'This is NOT funny, Charlotte,' and when I spun round in my seat to tell her to get the hell off me, I saw that she was trying not to cry and I realized it really wasn't funny. And then everything hit me at once and I realized too how tired I was and how much my head and stomach were hurting and how miserable and frightened and weird I felt and then I started to cry so hard that I thought I'd just go on crying forever and ever and DS Giles decided it would be better if he stopped the tape.

the skeLetONs iN mY CuPBOarD

They let me off with a warning. Before I was allowed out
of the interview room and able to walk, a free person, with
my mum down the steps of Cardiff Central Police Station, DS
Giles said, 'We'll be keeping an eye out for you, Charlotte. If
we ever see you in here again, you won't get off so lightly.'
So now I am under official surveillance by the South Wales
Police Force.

During the drive home my mum didn't speak at all, except
for once when she lowered her window and shouted at someone
who was driving in another car. I've never seen her do this
before. She is usually quite a calm person. I sat next to
her in the passenger seat and slid down as low as I could
without getting strangled by the seat belt. I would have slid
down and just disappeared altogether if I could. I wasn't
feeling very good.

When we got home I headed straight for the stairs because
I wanted to climb into my bed with all my clothes on and pull
the duvet up over my head and be on my own. I couldn't stand
the idea of my mum telling Ruthie and my dad about all of this,
and I didn't want to be able to overhear her on the phone
when she did. I especially hated the idea of Ruthie finding
out. I could just imagine her on the other end of a phone in
Aberystwyth, being all scandalized and wishing that she'd
never bothered to buy me that orang-utan T-shirt. I couldn't
bear to think about it. In fact, thinking about anything at all

was making me hideously miserable. Right then, I was really, really needing to be alone somewhere that was totally quiet and totally dark. To be honest, I even think that I wouldn't have minded dying all that much if I could have done it without any effort.

But when I was halfway up the stairs, my mum said, 'Oh no, you don't! You and I are going to sit down and have a talk.'

I didn't bother to argue. I felt so tired that there was no way I could have won anyway. I was pretty much a mess, to tell you the truth.[14]

When we were both sat down in the kitchen I braced myself and waited for my mum to go berserk. But she didn't. For ages she just sat there looking a bit old and a lot fed up and then, finally, she said, 'I think this is my fault.'

I looked up, surprised. Of all the things I had expected my mum to say, this was not one of them. I was so completely flabbergasted that for a minute or two I even forgot to feel miserable. I said, 'Er? Hello? I got caught nicking stuff. How can that possibly be your fault?'

My mum leaned her forehead against the palm of her hand and said, 'I haven't been paying you enough attention, and now you've gone completely off the rails. I should have seen this coming and stopped it.'

I sat there speechless. Making somebody feel angry is one

---

[14] I'm not all that great now.

thing but making somebody completely and utterly depressed is another thing altogether. It actually started to make me feel a bit cross. I looked my mum properly in the eye for the first time in days and days and said, 'I'm not a baby. I don't need twenty-four-hour childcare. Me stealing that stuff was my mistake. It's me that's messed up here, not you.'

My mum said, 'So why did you do it?'

And then I stopped feeling cross and shut up again because that was the question that had been confusing me all afternoon.

My mum said, 'Is this the first time you've taken things without paying for them?'

I scratched my thumbnail into the top of the table.

'Lottie, if we're going to put things right, we need to be honest with each other. I need to know everything NOW. I can't take any more surprises tomorrow or next week or next month. If you've got anything you need to tell me or any skeletons in your cupboard that need a good airing, I want them now, please.'

We sat in silence for a while and then I took a deep breath and said, 'I think I might have one or two other things in my wardrobe.'

My mum said, 'What are you trying to tell me, Lottie? You're going to have to speak up a bit — I can't hear you.'

So I took another deep breath and then I said,

'I think I might have one or two other things in my wardrobe.'

My mum nodded her head ever so slowly. 'We'd better go and take a look, hadn't we?'

Five minutes later my mum and I sat in silence on my bed and contemplated the scene in front of us. Covering the floor of my bedroom was an assortment of random items, some of which I clearly remembered seeing before and others of which I had no memory at all. All of them had come out of my wardrobe.

There was:

One pair of LAYLA ballet pumps in size four in black

One pair of LAYLA ballet pumps in size seven in
    brown

One copy of a book called Stevie Smith: A Critical
    Biography by Frances Spalding

Six cans of Heinz Baked Beanz

One pair of ETHEL indoor slippers in size five

Three packs of Melody Platinum Sun-kissed hair colorant

A roll of YOU PAY stickers

One copy of Shakespearean Sonnets

Twelve packs of American Tan tights

One pair of SHANE in size ten in fawn and brown

A pair of sunglasses

Four Sole Mates Shop Floor Sounds CDs

A left foot of an OLGA gym shoe in size three

A right foot of a TOPSY jelly shoe in size six

One copy of a book called Let's Speak Welsh

One Stevie Wonder CD, Songs in the Key of Life

One pair of CHARLOTTE ladies lace-ups in size six in
    beige
A plug-in air freshener
A toy giraffe
A James Dean mouse mat
A Forrest Gump DVD
A Dragon Coffee House mug (without any chips in it)
A birthday card (still in its plastic wrapping) with the
    words Happy Birthday Daughter on the front
A silver eyeshadow
A pair of foam insoles size seven to eleven
A key ring that looked like this:
and a £1 pack of fifty clothes pegs.

Gareth
(GW-reth)
Welsh origin
Meaning: Gentle

We sat there for ages, me and my mum,
just looking at all this stuff. Nobody was
more surprised than me at quite how
much of it there was. And most of it
was so scatty that it was almost funny in
a way. Almost.

   After a while, my mum said, 'Oh, Lottie!' And then she went
back to staring silently at my horde of stolen goods.

   I sat next to her and tried to work out in my head what
had happened. At first when my mum had opened the door of
my wardrobe and all this stuff had spilled out, I'd wanted to
deny all knowledge of it, say I'd never seen any of it before
in my entire life and blame the whole lot on a mystery burglar
who'd broken into our house, crept up to my bedroom and

hidden his entire stash of loot in my wardrobe. But as I looked at it, I started to see things that I definitely remembered taking. Things like the giraffe and the LAYLA ballet pumps and some of the tights, and then, the more I looked, the more I started to remember other stuff. Like taking the bus into town some days instead of going to school, and wandering round the bigger shops and picking things up and not necessarily putting them down again. And that was when I realized that I'd been doing a lot of stuff lately without properly thinking about it. It was like I had a lever in my head that only had two settings: INTENSE and AUTOPILOT. Half the time I was thinking too much and getting really deeply into stuff like selling tights and being Goose's friend and writing my English coursework, and the rest of the time I was spinning around doing a million things at once and thinking about NOTHING AT ALL. It was a very freaky realization.

I didn't know what to say so I just said, 'Am I grounded?'

My mum sighed and said, 'Yes, I'd say you probably are.'

We sat there quietly for a while and then I said, 'For how long?'

My mum shrugged her shoulders, sighed again and said, 'Until you're thirty-five.'

'Sorry,' I said and then, just because I was in trouble and it made me feel ever so slightly better, I started to rock a bit, and the sound my bed made was less a creak-thud kind of sound and more of an eek-eek kind of sound.

And do you know what? My mum still didn't shout at me.

Instead she put her arm round me and gave me a squeeze and said, 'It'll be OK, Lottie. We're going to sort this thing out, I promise you.'

And even though that was dead nice and understanding of her, it was also just about the most frightening thing I could have heard, because I think it was then that I started to have an inkling that there was really something very wrong with me.

hOw i LOst MY heaD fOr a MOmeNt But GOt MY COmPuter BaCk[15]

It is nineteen days since I last went to school, eighteen days since I was arrested and one day since a doctor told me that I am suffering from a mental disturbance of a reasonably significant nature.

To be honest, it's quite a big deal to get to grips with.

My mum is needing some time to adjust to this news as well. She hasn't been to work ever since she had to pick me up from the police station, and this is most unlike her. My mum is the type of person who has to be clinically dead before she'll take a sickie, and even then she'd probably go in for half the day until someone sent her home for being a public health and safety risk. Last night, I told her that she should go back to work because the criminal population of Cardiff must be causing total havoc

---

[15] Which, Mr(s) Examiner, I am sure you're delighted about, as my typing is a lot easier to read than my handwriting.

and chaos by now. My mum said, 'I'll go back to work when you are ready to go back to school. And anyway, they owe me some holiday time.'

I said, 'It hasn't been much of a holiday though, has it?'

And my mum smiled a bit then and agreed that no, it hadn't.

Because ever since that afternoon when me and my mum looked in my wardrobe, our lives have been well and truly and totally and utterly turned upside down. Instead of going to school, I've spent most of my time in bed and when I haven't been in bed I've been at the hospital answering billions of questions.

Quite a few times when I've been at home, the phone has rung and my mum has told me that Goose is desperate to speak to me but I've either pretended to be asleep or begged my mum to say that I'll call her back when I'm feeling better. So far I haven't called her back. It's not Goose's fault; it's just that I'm really NOT in the mood to speak to anyone at the moment. I think you could say that I've been having a series of EXTREME EXISTENTIAL DAYS.

I'm not making this all up to excuse myself for being a thief, by the way. I was caught red-handed and I've been officially told off for it. Fine. But the thing is, there actually IS something wrong with me, and it's as real and actual as mumps or chickenpox or whooping cough. Which brings me back to my earlier point:

I HAVE A MENTAL DISTURBANCE.

And this has been severely affecting my behaviour. Which, I think, is a relief in a funny kind of way. Sort of.

The day after I got arrested, I couldn't get out of bed. After days and days of either not needing or not being able to go to sleep, I suddenly found myself with the total opposite problem. It was like an OFF button had been flicked in my head. I couldn't stay awake. It wasn't like that Tuesday-morning feeling where I never want to get up because my bed is all warm and snugly and I've got double science with Mr Thomas first thing which means talking about amoebas for two hours; it was more serious than that. I couldn't have got out of my bed even if I'd woken up to find that I was sharing it with a particularly hungry, gigantic girl-eating spider and my life depended on it. Overnight I'd turned into a zombie. It felt like my brain had been kidnapped out of my head and replaced with a big cloud of soul-sucking smog. I'd become a bit like that old talking doll of mine, except that there was absolutely nothing funny about me. It's making me miserable just thinking about it.

My mum had barged into my bedroom at half past eight, opened up the curtains and said, 'You're not staying in bed all day. Your father is on his way down from Wrexham to talk to you.'

And I'd yawned a bit and cried a bit and then I'd just gone back to sleep, and when my dad showed up three hours later I could still barely keep my eyes open. And from somewhere, filtering faintly through the thick cloud of smog in my head, I heard my dad's voice say, 'This isn't normal, is it? I think she should see a doctor.' Pretty soon after that he went away again.

Then a really weird thing happened. I got it into my head that if I got out of bed, my house would collapse. I know this sounds seriously very strange but I honestly believed it would happen. I kept on having images of the roof caving in right on top of me just because I'd slammed a door too hard or thumped down the stairs a bit too heavily. Then I started imagining my house on the *Wales Today* news and it was just a great big pile of dusty rubble and all the neighbours were out on the street telling the reporters how sorry they were that me and my mum were still trapped underneath it all.

This freaked me out so much that I stayed in bed and didn't move except for when I absolutely desperately needed to go to the bathroom – and when that happened, I got really overanxious and started muttering, 'Please, God, don't let our house collapse . . . Please, God, don't let our house collapse . . . ' over and over again until I was safely back in bed.

I stayed in bed for the next four days, only getting up when I needed the bathroom. I didn't even eat or clean my teeth. Every now and then my mum barged in to try to steal the duvet off me, and I'd just cry and tell her I couldn't get up because our house was in serious danger of collapse. And then Dr Crosby appeared. I've known him all my life, but I wouldn't say that he is a friendly man, exactly. He's one of those people who always seems to be in a colossal hurry and doesn't really have time to talk. This time, though, it was a bit different. He sat on the chair next to my bed and said, 'What's all this about, Lottie? You know you can't stay in bed forever.'

I pulled the duvet up over my head and told him to shove off.

There was a short pause and then Dr Crosby said, 'Lottie, I have to ask you this: you haven't taken any drugs, have you? Cannabis? Magic mushrooms? Anything like that? I'm not going to have a go at you, I just need to know.'

Something about this question made me really cross. From beneath my duvet, I shouted, 'NO, I HAVEN'T ACTUALLY, THANK YOU VERY MUCH.'

There was another pause and then my mum said, 'She hasn't eaten anything since Saturday. She hasn't washed. She hasn't got dressed. She keeps crying. Quite honestly, she's frightening me.'

Underneath my duvet I pressed my hands hard over my ears. I could still hear them though.

Dr Crosby said, 'We've had similar episodes before, haven't we? Of course, it could just be adolescent depression. Sometimes a new hobby and a chat with one of our mental-health counsellors can be enough to get things back on track. But I think that Lottie really needs a more definite care plan. She has a history of these depressive episodes and it's important to understand that she may well need proper treatment to help get things under control.'

My mum said, 'I tried to make her see a counsellor last

year, but she wouldn't go.' Her voice was very quiet and a bit wobbly.

Dr Crosby said, 'Lottie, are you listening? I am going to arrange for you to see a specialist at the hospital who can help make you feel better. It's very important that you go.'

I said, 'But what about our house?

Dr Crosby said, 'Pardon?'

I pulled back my duvet a bit and said, 'What about our house? I just know that our house will collapse if I get out of bed.'

Dr Crosby looked at me for a long time and then he said, 'Your house is not going to collapse, Lottie.' For once he didn't sound too busy to talk to me. 'I'm going to arrange for you to see someone at the hospital as soon as possible, and when I've gone I want you to get dressed and try to have a little something to eat. Will you do that?'

I shrugged my shoulders. I really wasn't sure what I was going to do.

Dr Crosby and my mum left my room, but I could still hear them talking outside on the landing. Dr Crosby said, 'I'm going to organize a priority referral so that Lottie can be seen by a paediatric psychiatrist as soon as possible. It's very important she gets there.' And then he went downstairs and I couldn't hear any more.

The next day I was taken to see a doctor at the hospital. I'd eaten half a jacket potato and a few baked beans by then, but I still hadn't washed my face or cleaned my teeth. When we got to the hospital, me and my mum sat in a waiting room in front of a television which was showing a programme about little children dancing in a 'Baby Ballroom' competition. The whole thing did my head in so much that I started to cry again. I don't know why.

After several million hours a youngish woman with a smiley face and a pair of Adidas YOGA shoes on her feet touched me on the arm and said, 'Lottie? My name is Dr Edwards. Shall we have a chat in my room?'

I did a clockwork walk through the waiting room and into Dr Edwards's room. My mum put her hand across my back and did the clockwork walk with me.

Dr Edwards's room was small and untidy with cream walls. It reminded me a bit of the room where I had the interview at the police station. This time, though, there wasn't a tape recorder. Not one that I could see anyway. I sat down in a plastic chair and looked at the floor.

Dr Edwards said, 'Have you been feeling rotten, honey?'

I was so surprised that I stopped crying for a second and lifted my head up to look at Dr Edwards. She had one of those faces which can smile and look worried at the same time. All of a sudden, I desperately wanted her to help me.

'I'm a freak,' I said.

Dr Edwards smiled her nice, worried smile and then said, 'I must ask you, Lottie: have you taken any drugs? If you have, it would save a lot of time if you're honest with me.'

Instead of being cross, I said, 'I've never taken drugs ever. I don't need to. I'm going nuts all on my own.'

And then I started to cry again.

We stayed with Dr Edwards for quite a while. A lot of that time she spoke to my mum and sometimes she spoke to me, but I was feeling too terrible to talk much. If you want to know the truth, I was feeling a bit like I was a cartoon-scribble-person disappearing into a grey fog. Like this:

All the time she was talking, Dr Edwards tapped stuff into a computer on her desk. I could tell that she had a lot of private information about me on that computer. I could tell this because she knew all about the time I'd had to see Dr Crosby after I got excluded from school for trying to throw Samantha Morgan's desk out of the window.

After she'd finished talking and typing, she said, 'Lottie, it may not seem like it just yet, but you've made a big step towards getting better by coming here. What we need to do now is build as clear a picture of you as we can so that we're able to help you. You can help us by filling in this questionnaire, which will tell us exactly how you're feeling.'

It took me over an hour to fill in that questionnaire. Somebody brought me and my mum tea in plastic cups, but I barely touched mine. I was too busy trying to think. It reminded me a bit of those stupid questionnaires we sometimes have to fill in at school, except that this time there were no questions about how old I was – just loads and loads about how I felt. Questions like:

Place a tick in the column which best matches your response.	Yes, frequently	Yes, occasionally	Never
Do you laugh at inappropriate occasions?			
Do you have difficulty sleeping or problems with oversleeping?			
Have you experienced thoughts of death or suicide?			

It was a lot more interesting than the questionnaires we get given at school, but I can't say that it was fun exactly. When I'd finished, Dr Edwards told us to make another appointment for next week and then we went home.

When I went back the next week, Dr Edwards was wearing a pair of eighteen-hole Doc Martens on her feet, but other than that she was just the same as she'd been before and I was pleased to see her again. Me and my mum sat down in her room and she said, 'I've looked at all the information we have, Lottie, and that information, together with your past medical records, suggests very strongly that you are suffering from a mental disturbance of a reasonably significant nature.'

Me and my mum went very quiet.

Dr Edwards smiled her worried smile and said, 'What that means is that there is a medical reason why you've been feeling so up and down just lately. The episodes of unusual behaviour, the problems with sleeping, the recent depression ... these are all the results of a mental upset. What we need to do now is monitor the situation so that whatever it is that has been making you feel so terrible doesn't get any worse.'

I clapped my hand over my mouth and looked at the floor. I didn't know where to look. I definitely didn't want to look at my mum though.

Dr Edwards said, 'We see and help many, many people every week, Lottie, who are having to work through similar problems. It's a part of life. The mind is a complicated thing, and it's just as likely to have function difficulties as any other organ of the body. You can no more help having a mental upset any more than you can help having a high temperature or asthma or acne. The important thing to remember is that we are here to support you with this so that you can carry on going about your life successfully.'

Dr Edwards paused. Me and my mum continued to sit in silence on our plastic chairs. I noticed that my mum had taken hold of my free hand and was squeezing it, but I still couldn't bring myself to look at her face.

Dr Edwards said gently, 'I've asked you so many questions recently, Lottie. Is there anything that you'd like to ask me?'

I started biting my thumbnail. There were actually quite a few questions going around in my mind and I wasn't sure which one I wanted to ask first. After a moment or two I decided to ask the question that was worrying me the most.

'Are you saying that I'm a schizo?'

My mum made an exasperated noise and looked up at the ceiling. Dr Edwards leaned forward slightly in her chair and said, 'The answer is no, Lottie. I'm not saying that. Schizophrenia is an illness which leaves people feeling cut off from reality. They may hear voices that don't actually exist or they may see things that seem very real to them but actually aren't at all. You haven't presented us with any of these symptoms. If anything, it seems more likely that you may be suffering from some form of a mood disorder, which would account for the episodes of up and down behaviour you've had. There is something called bipolar disorder, or manic depression, which is diagnosed when it becomes clear that the individual has regular patterns of extreme elation and extreme depression, but—'

'Is that what Lottie has?' my mum asked.

Dr Edwards smiled at my mum and didn't seem to mind that she had been interrupted.

'The truth is, it's far too early for me or anyone else to be able to know *exactly* what the problem is—'

'But I'm definitely not a schizo?' It was me interrupting this time. I was really worried. Everybody at school calls Elvis Presley a schizo, and I didn't want them thinking I was going to end up like him.

Dr Edwards said. '*Schizophrenic* is the term I prefer, Lottie. I'm not sure that *schizo* is very polite − or actually has very much to do with schizophrenia.'

I saw my mum nodding.

'Sorry,' I whispered. For some reason I felt like I'd been told off even though Dr Edwards's eyes were still twinkling at me.

And anyway,' she added, 'even if it *did* become clear that you have a mild form of schizophrenia, we would help you to manage it.'

'Oh my God!' I said.

Dr Edwards reached forward and patted my hand. 'Don't worry, Lottie. We can sort this out. We have an adolescent centre set up to help young people just like you, and I'm going to get you talking to a counsellor there as soon as possible so that you can learn some ways to cope with your episodes of extreme or unusual behaviour.'

'How?' I asked.

Dr Edwards actually grinned. 'Well, that's a little question with a big answer. For now, let's just suggest that you try to focus as hard as you can on something nice whenever you start to feel a bit anxious or unhappy. But this is what a counsellor will be able to help you with. I'll also be seeing you on a regular basis to make sure everything is OK. To begin with, we'll see each other a fair bit but, all being well, I should soon be out of your hair before you know it.'

And then she gave me a really big smile – without any worry in it – and I was so relieved that, for some weird reason, I started to cry all over again. And finally, when my mum had finished asking the million-zillion questions that she wanted to ask, I said thank you to Dr Edwards and I made a promise to myself, right then and there, that I'd never use that stupid word schizo ever again.

When we got back home my mum surprised me by giving me my computer back. She asked me to help her bring it down from the loft and told me that she thought it might just cheer me up a little if I used it to keep a diary of how I'm feeling.

I told her that I don't do diaries. The only people I've ever heard of

Me-confused.

who kept them are Adrian Mole, who was a total geek-freak, and Anne Frank, who hid from the Nazis during World War II. And, quite frankly, Anne's problems totally kick mine into touch because her problems were hideously real, and mine are all in my head. That thought made me feel really guilty and ashamed all over again and, for the billionth time that day I started to cry. I'm surprised that Cardiff hasn't been issued with a flood warning.

My mum said, 'You don't *have* to write a diary, Lottie. For goodness sake, it was just a suggestion. Do whatever you want to do, so long as it cheers you up.' Then she gave me a kiss and went downstairs.

And the first thing I did, once my computer was safely reinstalled in my bedroom, was go on the Internet and see what I could find out about mental disturbances. There was a lot of information on there. Pages and pages. I started clicking on different sites and reading some of the stuff I found but most of it was quite boring and heavy and not the kind of stuff I wanted to read. I did learn one interesting thing though. In 1967 an American rock singer called Jimi Hendrix released the album *Are You Experienced?* and the second track on that album was called 'Manic Depression'. I remembered that this was one of the things Dr Edwards had mentioned, so I downloaded it on to my MP3 player and I've been pretty much solidly listening to it ever since. To be honest, it's not easy to hear what Jimi is saying because he does tend to howl quite a lot and there are also some seriously loud guitar noises to contend with – and I suppose I don't really know if Jimi Hendrix's 'experience' is anything like my experience anyway because I might not even *have* manic depression. But I do know that there is nothing shameful or embarrassing about that record. It is, without doubt, quite simply the COOLEST record I have EVER heard. Jimi's voice is, quite frankly, absolutely SEXADELIC and he uses it to tell the world about the mess he feels he's in.

And I don't think that even Stevie Smith or William Shakespeare could capture the essence of a mental disturbance of a reasonably significant nature any better themselves.

resurfaCiNG

Being a criminal outcast with a mental disturbance can be quite lonely. In the long space between my arrest and 3.45 this afternoon, I can honestly say that I saw pretty much nobody except my mum, my dad and a handful of random medical people. But since 3.45 that situation has changed. I have actually had a fairly hectic afternoon and now I am feeling quite socially exhausted. First of all, Goose came to visit me. It's not the first time that she's called for me this week. Today is Thursday and she has rung our bell at roughly twenty to four in the afternoon every day as she passes by on her way home from school. On Monday I made my mum tell her that I was asleep. On Tuesday we were late getting back from the hospital, and Goose had pushed a note through our letter box which read:

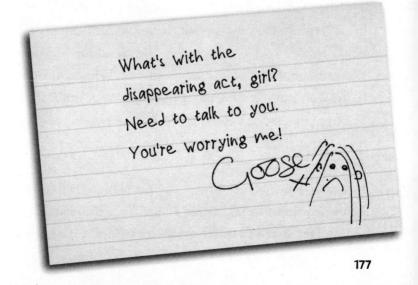

What's with the disappearing act, girl? Need to talk to you. You're worrying me!

Goose

Yesterday when she called, I was lying on my bed listening to Jimi Hendrix. My mum hammered on my bedroom door for ages and I had to turn the volume right up to maximum so that I couldn't hear her. Neither my mum nor Goose went away though. Outside my window the bell kept ringing as if Goose had got her finger surgically stuck to it, and outside my door my mum kept hammering with increasing violence until I thought she was going to knock the entire wall down. In the end she went downstairs and I lowered the volume of my MP3 player just in time to hear the front door open and my mum invite Goose in for a cup of tea. I crept to the top of the stairs then and curled myself up on the top step so that I could listen. They were talking in the kitchen for ages, but I couldn't hear what they were saying. It was probably about me, of course. Although, to be honest, there are a billion and one more interesting topics in the world to talk about. Even Gina is more interesting than I am.

When Goose eventually left, I dived back into my room before my mum came upstairs and knocked on my door again. This time I let her come in. She sat on my bed, pulled my earphones out of my ears and said, 'This is no good, Lottie. You can't keep yourself hidden away forever. It's not helping you, and it's not fair on Goose either. She's your friend and she's really worried about you. You've got to resurface at some point.'

I said, 'Since when have I been a blinking submarine?' Before my mum could answer, I added, 'Have you ever heard of Jimi Hendrix? His music totally rocks.' And then I put my earphones back in and pressed play. A minute or two later, my mum got up and left.

But at 3.45 this afternoon I turned off my MP3 player and faced the world again. I resurfaced. I didn't actually have any choice; Goose made me. I'd been lying on my bed, listening to Jimi, just like I'd been doing ever since Dr Edwards told me about my mental disturbance, when the bell rang again. I knew it would be Goose. I turned the volume up until the insides of my ears began to hurt, and I waited. A minute or two later my mum's head appeared around my bedroom door. I watched her pointlessly mouth some Hendrix-obliterated words and then I shut my eyes. When I opened them again, she was gone. I breathed a big sigh of relief and was just about to roll over and face my bedroom wall when, out of the very corner of my eye, I saw a sudden movement at my window. I sat up on my bed and stared. A second later, a stone bounced with a sharp crack against the glass. Then came another. And another. I ran over to the window and opened it. Outside, on our front lawn, Goose was scrabbling around on her hands and knees, picking stones out from beneath the rose bushes. I could see the top of her head very clearly and I was quite surprised to notice that she had some dark roots beginning to show through her Melody Forest Fire. Goose is usually very good at keeping her roots under control. I leaned out of the window and said, 'Stop it, Goose, you'll get an ASBO for doing that.' And then I said, 'Your roots are showing.'

Goose looked upward. 'Not as badly as yours are.' She raised her arm to show me something that she was holding and, weirdly, it was my alarm clock – the one which has been missing from my room for quite some time. 'I found this in the rose bush,' she said. 'Let me in, will you?'

I rested my elbows on the window ledge and sank my chin into my palms. 'I've been in trouble with the police,' I said.

Goose gave a shrug. 'I know that, Lottie. I was there when they came and arrested you.'

'And I've got a mental disturbance,' I said.

Goose shrugged again. 'I know that too. Your mum told me. Can I come in now?'

I stood there for a second, just looking out of the window and not really thinking about anything, and then I turned away and walked over to the door. At the bottom of the stairs I nearly collided with my mum, who was coming out of the kitchen and into the hall. When she saw me she stopped, looked a bit surprised and then turned round and went right back into the kitchen. I opened the front door and let Goose in.

Once we were upstairs Goose said, 'I want you to know that I've resigned from Sole Mates. I've been feeling really bad, Lottie. Honestly I have.'

I looked at her surprised. I was actually slightly put out, if I'm honest. I know there aren't exclusive rights to these things, but if there were, it felt as if losing a Saturday job and feeling bad were pretty much my own personal specialities. I

didn't need Goose to muscle in on the act. I pulled my best miserable face

and asked, 'Why?'

Goose hugged her knees tightly, looked a bit sad and said, 'It's my fault, isn't it? I started it all when I said it would be OK to rescue those stupid ESMERELDA shoes. I wasn't rescuing anything though, was I? I was stealing. Well, I took them back and told Dionne I was resigning. She said she didn't want me to leave, but *I* wanted to. To be honest, Lotts, I didn't want to be stuck there with Emily and Gina and without you anyway. Who would? You'd have to be completely stark raving mad to want to work with those two.'

As soon as Goose had said this, she went bright red, clapped her hand over her mouth and gave me a muffled apology.

In spite of myself, I smiled. She was right. You *would* have to be mad to want to work in a shoe shop with Emily the Shameless Man-Snatcher and Gina who has never known true love. She was wrong about the other thing though. I pulled her hand away from her mouth, locked my fingers with hers and said, 'S'not your fault, Goose. I had half of Cardiff stashed in my wardrobe. I suppose it wasn't absolutely

---

[16] This is Victoria, Queen of England and Empress of India. Which just goes to show that money really *can't* buy you happiness.

my fault either. I've been kind of ill. I'm going to be OK though. They're going to teach me how to stop being mental.'

Goose squeezed my fingers. 'What does it feel like?'

It was a good question. I had to think for quite a while before I could answer her. Finally I said, 'I feel like I've fallen down a manhole, if you know what I mean.'

Goose said, 'Not really.'

So then I got off my bed, crossed over to my desk and picked up a piece of paper and a pen. On it I drew another one of those Scream pictures, except that this time, I put my own head on it.

When I'd finished, I climbed back on to my bed and showed it to Goose. She puffed out her cheeks and looked at it for quite a long time, then said, 'I think I get it now.'

We sat in silence for a little while, side by side on my bed, with our backs to my bedroom wall. It didn't matter that we weren't saying much; it was quite nice just to have somebody near me who wasn't mad at me and who didn't think that I was mad – at least, not in a bad way. Eventually Goose said, 'Do you think *I've* got a mental disturbance?'

I laughed then. I actually laughed right out loud, and it was a *proper* laugh, not a weird laugh. I said, 'It's not like a cold, Goose. You can't catch it from me.'

Goose went all red again. 'No, I do know that, thank you, Lottie. It's just that, well, I have existential days, don't I? Sometimes I can be *well* miserable. Maybe I've got a problem with my head. How do you know that I haven't?'

This was another good question. I shrugged my shoulders and said, '*Everybody* has crap days, Goose. Life isn't all funny ha ha, is it? It's just that my crap days have been so crap just recently that it feels like my brain has bust. I think that's the difference.'

'Yes, but how do I *know*?' said Goose. 'How depressed do you have to be?'

This time *I* puffed out my cheeks and had a long think. Eventually I said, 'Well, have you ever found yourself wishing that you were someone else?'

Goose's eyes went really wide and her mouth opened up in a big circle of shock.

'Oh my God, Lottie, all the time!!!

I'm *always* wishing I was somebody else. I'd *much* rather be Cameron Diaz than me. Does that mean I'm ill? Oh . . . My . . . God.' Goose laid her hands flat against her cheeks and shook her head with one hundred per cent genuine alarm before adding, 'Sometimes I wouldn't mind being a female

Marilyn Manson either. I know he's not conventionally attractive, but he has got beautiful eyelashes.'

I laughed again. I was turning into a laugh a minute, I really was. 'No, Goose. You don't get it. Most people want to be someone famous at some point but, well, do you ever have that feeling that you are so completely rubbish that there are times you'd rather be *anyone* else.' I stopped laughing and started feeling sad again. 'I mean, even Gina, for example.'

Goose took her hands away from her cheeks and stared at me. When she spoke her voice was nearly a whisper. 'Gina? God, no!'

I gave her a sad smile. 'Well, I suppose that's the difference between being a bit mental and just being a bit pissed off.'

Goose nodded and looked at the floor. She was clearly a bit shocked. I picked up my MP3 player, pushed the earphones into her ears and said, 'Listen to this. It's totally banging.' And then I played 'Manic Depression' and introduced her to the amazing world of Jimi Hendrix. I needed to lighten the mood.

what ¡ LearNeD whiLe ¡ was iNsiDe the warDrOBe

Goose stayed for nearly two hours before heading off home to get her tea. She'd barely been gone twenty minutes when the doorbell rang again. At first I thought that it was just Goosey coming back again to ask if she could burn a CD from my Jimi Hendrix download, but then I heard a voice downstairs and it wasn't Goose's voice. It was Dionne's.

Dionne.

My ex-manageress.

Whose shop I had been BLATANTLY thieving from.

My face went straight from this

to this.

I entered a state of total and utter shock. Not even Cerys, my dead bunny, could have been any more shocked when she looked up that day and saw a greedy great kestrel hanging over her head. And then my mum called up the stairs, 'Lottie! Can you come down, please? You've got another visitor.'

I really didn't know what to do so, for a moment, I just stood on my back legs in the middle of my room with my ears all alert and a look of panic all over my furry little face. And then, just as my mum reached the top of the stairs, I legged it across my room and shut myself in my wardrobe.

It was quite nice inside there. It was all dark and snug and smelt ever so slightly of fust. Normally I would not expect to enjoy the smell of fust, but it's quite nice so long as it's strictly your own fust. I suppose I felt pretty much how a rabbit must feel when it's all safe and sound inside its burrow. If I could have done, I probably would have stayed there inside my wardrobe forever.

But then my mum knocked on my bedroom door and said, 'Lottie!'

Inside my wardrobe I curled up into a tight ball and stopped breathing. I heard my bedroom door open and the sound of my mum's footsteps as she came into my room. There was a bit of a pause and then she said, 'Lottie?'

I still didn't move and I still didn't breathe.

From the other side of my wardrobe door, I heard a bit of shuffling as my mum moved around my room and then she screamed, 'THE WINDOW! OH MY GOD! LOTTIE!'

and there was the sound of her blatantly legging it across my bedroom.

And then I remembered that my window was still wide open from when I'd been talking down to Goose in the front garden, and I don't mind telling you that it made me feel truly totally terrible because I realized that, for one horrible second, my mum *actually* must have thought I'd thrown myself out of it.

I stopped holding my breath and coughed. The noises outside stopped. Then, in the most normal voice that I could manage, I said, 'It's OK, mum. I'm in the wardrobe.'

There was another pause and then my mum said, 'Why?'

'I'm not coming out until you make Dionne go away,' I said.

My mum opened my wardrobe door. With daylight back and my mum's face frowning down at me, I no longer felt like a bunny safe in a burrow. I just felt stupid.

'Lottie, Dionne wants to talk to you, and I think you should listen to what she has to say. And NO, I am not going to send her away,' said my mum.

'Well, I'm staying here then,' I said, and pulled the door closed again.

Outside my mum made a hissy cross sound. It was the first hissy cross sound I'd heard her make in ages. I was quite hurt by it, to be honest. But maybe a bit relieved too.

'Fine!' she said. 'I'll send Dionne up here then and she can talk to you while you're in the wardrobe.'

'You wouldn't dare!'

'Wouldn't I? Watch me.'

And then I heard my mum walk out to the landing and call down in a loud voice, 'Would you like to come up, Dionne? My fifteen-year-old daughter is inside her wardrobe.'

And to my total and utter SHAME and HORROR, Dionne came up the stairs and into my BEDROOM. I was

STUPENDOUSLY

furious with my mum, but I was also still inside my wardrobe so there wasn't really very much I could do about it.

I opened the door a micro-fraction and peeked through the gap. Dionne was standing in the middle of my room. Her hair was Melody Platinum Sun-Kissed. It always is. Unlike me and Goose, Dionne doesn't have the sort of dynamic personality which can carry off frequent changes of hair colour. She's a nice person though. I watched her as she stood there staring in the direction of me and the wardrobe. She'd brought her hands up to her mouth and pressed them flat together and, for a split second, I thought she was praying. But then I saw that she was nervously chewing the tops of her fingernails. My guess is that she'd never spoken to a mad person in a wardrobe before. After a minute or two, she got down and knelt on the floor. Inside my wardrobe I muttered, 'Make yourself at home, why don't you?' and then I braced myself for a full-on lecture session about the badness of being a thief.

Dionne cleared her throat. 'Lottie, I wanted to come and see you. I've been quite worried about you, to be honest.

Gina told me what happened and, um, it's obviously not good, but it seems very out of character. And then yesterday Goose told me that you've not been too well. And, er, I want you to know that I think that probably explains quite a lot.' Through the gap in my door I saw Dionne pause just long enough to bite the thumbnail on her left hand. 'I want you to know that I'm not angry with you.'

I didn't know what to say so I didn't say anything.

Dionne cleared her throat again. 'Lottie, I do understand that things aren't always as clear-cut as they seem. Um, the thing is, I knew this girl once – you remind me of her quite a lot, actually – and she had lots of friends and was doing so well at school and everything and then, in her teens, she just went completely off the rails for apparently no reason.'

This wasn't the kind of thing that I'd been expecting at all. I'd been expecting her to tell me I was horrifically disgraceful and that I should be publicly flogged and then thrown off the flyover. Inside my wardrobe, I stopped feeling stupendously furious with my mum and started to feel stupendously confused instead.

Dionne gave a big sigh. 'This girl I knew, she started getting in trouble at school and was rowing a lot with her parents, and everyone thought that she was a troublemaker. Eventually she even got thrown out of school. And the thing is, Lottie, the more trouble she got in, the more depressed she felt. I suppose what nobody realized was that she was just very, very unhappy with who she was, and getting into trouble was a way of waving at the world and saying, "Hello, everyone, I'm over here. Will somebody please come and help me."'

I opened my door a fraction more and looked at Dionne's face as she spoke. I'd never actually heard her say that much before because, usually she just keeps herself shut away in the office of Sole Mates and organizes her hectic social life. This new chatty side to her personality was a bit of a revelation. I still wanted her to leave though so I said, 'Yeah, whatever, but I don't actually want my job back.'

Dionne looked surprised. 'Well, that's good because I haven't come here to offer you your job back. Much as I like you, I don't think you should be working anywhere just at the moment. I've got a shop to run, remember, and whatever the problem might be, you've still been nicking enough shoes from me to kit out a millipede.' She paused and then said, 'Are you gonna come out of that wardrobe?'

'I doubt it,' I said.

Dionne smiled to herself. 'Well, in that case, I won't stay long, Lottie. I just wanted to tell you that this girl I knew, she went through such a bad time when she was a teenager that she even ran away for a while. But that didn't help either because the thing that she was trying to run away from was this bad feeling inside her head. She could have gone to Disneyland or the Bahamas even and she'd still have done bad things and got into trouble because she had this horrible, miserable feeling trapped in her head and she couldn't make it go away. In the end the police found her and brought her home. And by then her head was in such a state that finally everyone realized that there was something seriously wrong and got her some help.'

Dionne stood up. 'Anyway, the reason I'm telling you all this is because that girl I knew would have felt a whole lot better if she'd known that she wasn't the only person in the world who suffered from that kind of problem.'

And then she smiled to herself again, a bit sadly this time, and walked towards my bedroom door.

'Dionne?' I opened the door of the wardrobe and clambered out. Dionne had paused at the top of the stairs.

'Dionne – what happened to that girl? Was she all right in the end?'

Dionne's face brightened. 'Yes, she was actually. For a while, she was given pills to help control her moods, but pretty quickly she decided that she didn't want to be taking them forever so she learned how to spot when a bad mood was coming so she could control it by herself. And now I'm really happy to say that she's almost always in a good mood and has loads of fantastic mates and is out partying with them nearly every weekend – and if she *does* have a bad mood, she just keeps her head down until it passes and eats custard slices for a bit of a boost. And she manages a shoe shop. And she's only twenty-two. That's not bad, is it?'

And then she gave me a wave of the hand and turned and went downstairs.

I was about to climb back into the wardrobe and think about this when my mum's voice floated up from the hallway and stopped me in my tracks.

'Thanks for stopping by and having a chat with her, Dionne. That was really good of you,' she said.

'I wanted to,' replied Dionne. 'Goodbye, Sergeant Biggs.'

And then I heard the front door close. I don't mind admitting that I was mightily weirded out by that little exchange. I had absolutely NO IDEA that my mum and Dionne knew each other. My mum has never ever once mentioned it and neither has Dionne. How totally random is that?

a Break iN the CLOuDs

Dionne had barely been gone twenty minutes when the doorbell rang again. I had no idea who it could be pressing the button this time and I was too worn out to bother guessing, but I felt certain that whoever it was had stopped by to visit me; for some reason, I suddenly seemed to be getting more visitors than the Pope. I wasn't taking any chances though so I ran to the top of the stairs and shouted, 'Mum, if it's Gina and you let her in, I WILL throw myself out of the window. I'm just telling you that now so you know.' And then I got back in the wardrobe and closed the door.

Wardrobes are handy things. They are blatantly very useful for keeping your clothes in and if, like me, you have a big wardrobe and a small body, they are also extremely accommodating places to hide. Especially if you are fifteen years old. Nobody would ever think to look for a fifteen-year-old inside a wardrobe.[17] Wardrobes are not, however, any good if you want to keep track of what's going on in the wider world. Unless people are either shouting or in the same room, you can't actually hear anything much of what's going on. For a few minutes I sat curled up in the silent fusty darkness of my wardrobe, waiting for whoever had rung the bell to come barging into my bedroom without an invitation, and while I sat in there I started praying, over and over again,

---

[17] Except my mum, who knows what I'm like.

in an urgent little whisper, and what I was praying was this:

'Please, God, don't let it be Gina. Please, God, don't let it be Gina. Please, God, don't let it be Gina. Please, God, don't let it be Gina. Please, God, don't let it be Gina. Please, God, don't let it be Gina. Please, God, don't let it be Gina.'

And I really, really desperately meant it, because the possibility that Gina might walk into my room at any second had forced me to think through the decision to throw myself out of the window if she did. And, actually, however bad I'd been feeling recently, I didn't think that I really seriously wanted to do it. But I still wasn't sure so I started to make a list in my head of all the reasons why I might – and that list looked like this:

Reasons For Jumping Out of the Window
I won't have to face Gina.
My mum can go back to work.
I won't have to go to any more double-science lessons ever
    again.
I'm too short anyway.
I've got a stupid nose.
I am a thief.
I've got mental problems.

This list made me feel fairly depressed to be honest and, for a moment or two, I thought that maybe I'd convinced myself and that was that, but then I remembered that there are always two sides to every argument so I started to make another list and that list went like this:

Reasons Against Jumping Out of the Window
My mum will be sad forever.
So will Ruthie.
So will my dad.
So will Goose.
Gareth Stingecombe might be for a little while as well.
I haven't finished my English coursework yet and I think I might get an A★.
The school disco is a week next Friday and I'm not 100% sure that I don't want to go.
I've only just discovered the music of Jimi Hendrix. I might discover other stuff.
My nose might be stupid but the rest of me is OK.
Kylie Minogue is even shorter than I am and it doesn't bother her.
Madonna isn't all that tall either and she's a billionaire pop bitch.
I haven't yet had a sexual experience.
I want to show the world that I am no longer, and never again will be, a thief.
I'll miss loads of art lessons.
I want to go into the sixth form and get some A levels.
I want to see orang-utans in the wild.
I'd also quite like to ride on a camel.

I wouldn't want to die with my roots showing.

A reasonably significant mental disturbance is nothing to be ashamed of.

Me and Goose have an outrageously funny time sometimes.

Double choco-mochaccinos.

Most of my teachers like me so I can't be all that horrific.

Gareth Stingecombe likes me.

Even Dionne said she likes me and I stole her tights.

Charlotte Beryl Biggs must be all right really, I reckon.

And when I'd finished this list, I sat curled up in the fusty silent darkness of my wardrobe and, for the first time in absolutely ages, my face was properly like this:

And it was a seriously happy face.

I sat there in my wardrobe, just letting all this good stuff roll around inside my head and it felt really cosy and nice. Whichever way I looked at it, the second list made so much more sense than the first that it just completely blew that first list to pieces. It felt so good that I forgot all about the fact that Gina was quite possibly about to barge her way into my bedroom at any moment and I just sat there, smiling to myself, in the dark. And it was so quiet and I felt so tired after all that chit-chat with Goose and Dionne, and it was so perfectly peaceful in my fusty old wardrobe, that I just closed my eyes and without even realizing that it was happening, I drifted off and fell sound asleep. And the next time I opened my eyes it was because someone had opened the door of the wardrobe and put her arms around me and was giving me a big squeeze. And that person was my sister Ruthie. She gave me a kiss and whispered, 'What's been bugging you then, fart face?'

I was so chuffed and so relieved because, at last, it felt like the sun had properly come back out in my head.

the writiNG ON the waLL

On this day, Monday 14 July, I, Charlotte Beryl Biggs, aged fifteen years and almost one month, of 62, Springfield Place, Whitchurch, Cardiff, Wales, United Kingdom, Europe, Planet Earth, The Universe, left my house and boldly ventured

BACK TO SCHOOL.

In no way was it easy, but it was definitely positively the right thing to do. My mum wanted me to stay at home because there is only one more week of term before the summer break, but Dr Edwards said that I should try to go in if I could because otherwise starting school again in September after such a long gap could just feel like a total freaking nightmare. And besides, I really need to catch up with my schoolwork because I've got important exams next summer and I want to get into the sixth form to study English, history and art. After that I've decided that I'd quite like to go to university and do a degree in writing because I've learned a lot about myself in the last month or so and one of the nicer things I've learned is that writing is something which I actually enjoy doing very much. Ruthie says that I'd probably like it at Aberystwyth University because it's chilled-out and friendly and by the sea and loads of interesting people live there. I asked her to name one of them but she couldn't. My mum says I should stay in Cardiff where she can keep an eye on me. I've been doing some research and I've decided that

I'd like to go to the island of Jersey because it has a wildlife foundation which has a very large and happy collection of orang-utans rescued from situations of danger all over the world but mostly from Sumatra. If I studied in Jersey, I'd be able to go and watch them swing around as often as I liked.

When I told my mum and Ruthie this, Ruthie laughed and said, 'Duh! I think you'll find that there isn't actually a university in Jersey, fart face.'

My mum said, 'Ruthie, WILL you STOP calling her that!' and then she said, 'Don't worry, Lottie, you've got a few years yet to decide anyway.'

And I suppose that was when I really knew that I was feeling a whole lot better because thinking about the future seemed OK and didn't make my brain melt.

Ruthie was still around this morning and walked to school with me and Goose. When we got to the gates she gave me a big hug and said, 'Be brave today, Lottie, and when you're feeling absolutely better I promise that you can come up to stay in Aber one weekend and meet all my archaeology friends.'

I said, 'BIG WOW! That sounds positively thrilling, fish breath.' And then I gave her a big hug back and went into school with Goose.

It was well weird being back there. Well weird. I'd just had three whole weeks off school and, apart from that time when I was seven and broke my leg, I've never had three weeks off in one go ever. Normally my mum likes me to be certifiably dead before she'll let me stay off for more than three days in a row. Three weeks away felt like forever. Everybody I saw in the corridor looked different. They'd got bigger and grown longer hair and swapped spots and stuff. Melvyn Pugh had even developed a moustache – sort of – and he's only four foot ten. I don't mind admitting that, as I walked into the main building, the whole scene was making me quite nervous and edgy. Even so, I was feeling nowhere near as nervous and edgy as I'd been feeling just a week ago. It might sound weird, but knowing that I have an ACTUAL PROPER PROBLEM which doctors can help me fix has cheered me up a lot. Before that, I just thought I was going nuts.

The day didn't get off to a very good start. I was a bit worried about going on my own to registration, but then Goose said she'd come along with me even though she's not in my form. Luckily my form tutor is Mrs Peebly. I haven't mentioned her before because she's completely pointless and about as useful as a holey bucket. Being this useful does have the potential to be supremely annoying, but on this occasion it was actually fairly handy because Peebly didn't notice that Goose wasn't supposed to be there. I'm not sure that Peebly actually even understands why she has to go to registration herself. Most of the time Beca Bowen has to remind her to take the register. Another thing about Mrs Peebly is that she has these funny eyes that look in two different directions both at once so that you can never be too sure who she is looking at. She is not a very good form tutor, but she would make an excellent spy.

When we walked in Mrs Peebly sort of looked at us and also at the wall behind us and said, 'Good morning, girls,' and then, sort of looking at me but not looking at me, she said, 'Bethan, you need to see the year tutor at break-time.' I paused in front of Mrs Peebly's desk and said, 'I'm Lottie Biggs.' Mrs Peebly turned her head to the right a bit, looked Goose full in the face and said, 'Yes, I know, dear. I hope you're feeling better. I was talking to Bethan.' I just smiled then and nodded and moved quickly out of the way. Goose did too. Sometimes it's for the best.

Me and Goose walked over to the emptiest corner of the room and sat down. I was feeling a bit freaked out. It wasn't just the random weirdness of conversational exchanges with Mrs Peebly that had done it; there was a whole load of stuff making my head boggle. Stuff like:

Why are school corridors painted the colour of cat sick?

Why would anyone want to stick chewing gum to the ceiling?

Why do boys Tipp-Ex pictures of penises on to chairs?

Why do I then have to sit on those chairs?

Why do all classrooms smell like pet shops?

Why don't any of the windows open?

Why does Lee Fogel eat pizza at half past eight in the morning?

Why has someone written *THIS DESK IS GAY* on my desk?

Why does Mrs Peebly wear such nasty shoes?[18]

Why do we have to sit in form rooms doing nothing for fifteen minutes every morning?

Why can't we just begin every day with double art?

Like I said before, WELL WEIRD.

To be honest, I don't reckon it's worthwhile wasting too much energy trying to find the answers to these questions because I don't think that there actually are any. Some things about life make no sense whatsoever and you just have to do your best to operate around them. This is something I am learning. So I sat down with Goose and tried not to think about any of this. Besides, it was way too deep for 8.35 in the morning. Instead I tried to relax a bit before art. But I'd barely been sat there, trying to relax, for more than a nanosecond before Gareth Stingecombe saw me and boomed at the very top of his voice, 'Biggsy!' Then, before I even knew what was happening, he'd pulled me up out of my seat, lifted me right off the ground and swung me round in a big bear hug. I think he mistook me for a rugby ball. Goose coughed and said, 'Gareth! Lottie's been ill, you muppet.' Gareth Stingecombe put me down then, held out his hand for me to shake and said, 'Good to have you back with us, Biggster.' Gareth Stingecombe can be quite weird as well, sometimes.

---

[18] Could they really be CHARLOTTE ladies lace-ups in brown? Yes, I think they could!

He's OK though.

After Gareth had wandered off, I tried again to concentrate on being calm and peaceful. It was tricky. At the back of the classroom, Lee Fogel had finished his pizza and was shouting his mouth off about some amazing goal he'd scored at the weekend. He wouldn't shut up. He's got a very loud voice. He sounds like a radio which is constantly tuned to STUPID FM. I was really doing my best to ignore him by thinking about orang-utans and other calming nice stuff, and I was doing quite well until Lee took a football out of his bag and kicked it in a woeful attempt to recreate the goal he was boasting about. The ball shot across the room and smacked me hard on the side of the head. Mrs Peebly, who, as I may have mentioned, is about as useful as a chocolate teapot, looked in the wrong direction and squeaked, 'Lee, put that ball away and apologize to Lottie, please.'

Lee Fogel laughed.

Goose jumped up out of her chair and said, 'Oi, Fogel! Watch what you're doing, you numpty!'

In a slightly delayed reaction, which I can only assume was due to post-traumatic stress, I put my hand to my head and said, 'OWW!'

Lee Fogel walked across the room, picked up his ball and said to Goose, 'What's she going to do about it? *Steal my trainers?*'

And then he turned around and started swaggering back across the classroom with his ball tucked under his arm. I don't like him much.

Goose went bright red and opened her mouth to say something, but whatever she was about to say was lost forever. Instead, from the back of the classroom, Gareth Stingecombe's voice boomed out:

'FOGEL! APOLOGIZE!'

I'll say one thing for Gareth. Apart from being very good at rugby and having very big feet and colossal manly thighs and quite a nice face, he also has an exceptionally powerful voice. When he wants to, Gareth Stingecombe can be even louder than Lee Fogel. One boom from Gareth and all other conversation in the classroom stopped. Everyone turned to look at him. And then they looked at Lee Fogel. And then they looked at me.

I suddenly started to feel really sick.

For a split second Lee Fogel looked a bit confused, and then he shrugged his shoulders and said, 'What's the matter, Gaz? It was a top header from a top headcase.' And then he looked at me and grinned and said, 'Nice header, *schizo.*'

And then something very freaky happened. Everyone in the classroom seemed to freeze except for me. It was like they were all actors in some DVD rental film and a giant person on the other side of the screen had pressed the pause button so that they could go out to the kitchen and make a cup of tea. The only person who wasn't rooted to the spot was me.

I sat there, trapped in this frozen scene from a bad film,

and looked at the characters around me. Goose's face was thunderous. She looked every bit scary enough to be the lead singer in a goth-rock band called Destiny of Death. She looked scarier even than Marilyn Manson, and that takes some doing because he looks like this:

Lee Fogel was laughing lamely but, at the same time, blatantly backing away from Gareth Stingecombe, who looked like he was about to rip Lee's arms and legs off. Mrs Peebly, who is about as useful as a holiday home on Mars, was staring anxiously in two directions at once, but whether she had spotted the bloody violence that was about to break out at any second between Lee Fogel and Gareth Stingecombe was anyone's guess. And in the middle of all this was me. Before I had time to ponder on this tricky situation any further, everyone started to move again and Gareth Stingecombe's voice boomed across the room once more. It sounded like the noise a volcano probably makes just before it blows its top and kills everyone.

'FOGEL! TAKE THAT BACK AND APOLOGIZE!'

And I understood then that Gareth Stingecombe didn't just sound like a volcano which was about to blow, he WAS a volcano which was about to blow, and there was a very real and distinct danger that he might kill Lee Fogel in the process. And although I don't like Lee Fogel very much, I do quite like Gareth Stingecombe and I didn't want him to get into serious trouble on my account. So I took a deep, deep breath and stood up and said, 'It's all right, Gareth. I don't want an apology.' And then I turned to Lee Fogel, who was trying to smirk and appear cool but actually just looked as if he had an internal problem with trapped wind and said, 'I *did* nick some shoes, Lee, and some other stuff, and I wish I hadn't. But *you* needn't worry because there's no way I'm going to steal your trainers or anybody else's because I'm totally through with all of that. And besides, I can smell your trainers from here and they're pretty minging – so I really don't think you actually need to worry about *anyone* making off with them.'

Lee opened his mouth to say something but I was in full flow. And I had an audience now so I thought I'd better make it count.

'And while we're at it, I'm not a schizophrenic. But seeing as you brought the subject up, schizophrenia is an illness which leaves people feeling totally cut off from reality. That must be pretty scary and horrible, I reckon. And I don't think it's nice to laugh at someone because you think they might be ill and scared. That's quite pathetic and nasty, actually!'

And then, without even bothering to ask Mrs Peebly,

who is about as useful as an Oompa-Loompish dictionary, I picked up my bag, marched straight out of the room and down the corridor to the girls' toilets. I didn't need the loo or anything – I just needed a moment on my own to clear my head and calm myself down away from everyone else.

At the end of the corridor I almost bumped into Mrs Rowlands, the Welsh teacher. I have always had a sneaking suspicion that she hates me. This has been based on the evidence of all the rubbish marks I am consistently given for my Welsh homework and the fact that it was her who got me excluded in Year 9 for throwing Samantha Morgan's exercise book and bag out of the window. But I only did it because she called my mum a rozzer and I thought she'd said lezzer. Thinking about that now, it all sounds a bit stupid, but at the time it made me flip out at 7.0 on the Richter scale.[19] I would have thrown Samantha's desk out of the window as well, but it was too big and I ended up smashing the glass a bit and then Mrs Rowlands used her mobile phone to get the Head of Year to come and take me away and after that Samantha Morgan's mum told Samantha not to speak to me any more.

It therefore came as an enormous surprise to me when Mrs Rowlands stopped, smiled and said, 'Hello Lottie. Good to have you back!' And then she patted me on the arm and carried on down the corridor. I was so confused and startled

---

[19] 7.0 = A **great** earthquake which is capable of causing serious damage over a large area. (I got this out of Mr Thomas's science book. ☺)

that, for a second, I froze right there in the corridor with my mouth open. I can only explain Mrs Rowlands's action in the following ways:

1. She does not hate me and she is actually quite nice. And to be fair, I suppose it was a bit off-putting when I tried to throw that desk out of the window.
2. She also has a mental disturbance and is currently in an *up* mood.

Either way, it was nice of her.

Inside the toilets, I was relieved to find that there was nobody else around. I walked over to the furthest cubicle, pulled down the toilet lid and sat on it with my head in my hands and shut my eyes. My head was bouncing about like a space hopper and I really needed to escape school for a moment by thinking of something nice like orang-utans to help calm it down. I sat there on the loo, concentrating as hard as I could on a mental image of their sweet ginger faces, but, for some reason, my brain wasn't having any of it. Instead the only thing I could think about was how Gareth Stingecombe had got so upset on my account.

After a little while, I opened my eyes again and looked up. On the back of the door, somebody had written:

I sat on the lid of the toilet and stared. Then I leaned a little closer to the door and checked to see that I'd read it correctly. I had. It was my name. I am the only person called Lottie Biggs in my school.

I sat back on the toilet lid and just kept on staring at the door. Seeing my name on it had surprised me so much that my brain had stopped bouncing around and was doing ABSOLUTELY NOTHING AT ALL.

I leaned down and rummaged in my bag. I pulled a marker pen out of my pencil case, stood up and made an adjustment to what was written on the back of the toilet door.

And then I sat back down on the toilet lid again and considered this new message. It was definitely a more positive message. And there was blatantly some truth in it. After all, I'm not exactly mad; it's more like Dr Edwards said – I am having some functioning difficulties of the mind.

I was about to put my pen away when a random thought made me pause. It was quite a complex and deep random thought. In actual fact, I'm not sure that I have ever had such a complex and deep random thought ever before in my life and I'm not at all sure that I ever will again. It was this.

What exactly does mad mean anyway?

Don't get me wrong, I'm not stupid. I know what the word mad *means*[20], but what I don't understand is WHO DECIDES what is or isn't mad behaviour. I mean, I'm not trying to wriggle out of this and say that my behaviour just recently has been perfectly normal and OK because blatantly it hasn't, but what I'm trying to say is, however mad I may have been acting is no more randomly weird than the behaviour of this person who writes stupid pointless things on the backs of toilet doors. I may have my moments, but I'm not *that* mad. Not yet anyway. I took the lid off my pen again, stood up and made another adjustment.

And then I put my pen back in my pencil case, picked up my bag and left. I don't mind telling you that I was smiling. I reckon the best proof of sanity is being able to identify a bit of madness in yourself and be OK with it.

---

[20] **măd** *adjective* 1. having something wrong with the mind; insane; 2. extremely foolish; 3. very keen.

CONfrONtiNG CertaiN seNsitive issues heaD ON

I think the rest of the day went fairly well. In a funny-peculiar way, Lee Fogel calling me a schizo actually helped. It forced me to confront the sensitive issue of my illness head on and deal with it. I am very proud of myself. My calm response to the situation was probably the BEST thing I could have done to prove to everyone at school that I, Lottie Biggs,

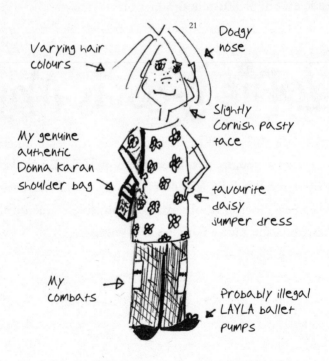

21

Varying hair colours →

Dodgy nose

Slightly Cornish pasty face

My genuine authentic Donna Karan shoulder bag →

favourite daisy jumper dress

My combats →

Probably illegal LAYLA ballet pumps

---

[21] This drawing is not to scale.

am actually a **SUPREMELY INTELLIGENT AND MATURE HUMAN BEING** AND it also gave me the opportunity to tell Lee Fogel that his trainers ming.

Anyway, I was so buzzed up by this blatant moral victory that I decided I was going to tackle a few more sensitive issues head on and DEAL WITH THEM. Here they are:

1. The Sensitive Issue of my Unhealthy Art Obsession with Edvard Munch

All of this entire term, I have been working in my art lessons on a 150cm x 80cm reproduction, in felt-tips, of Edvard Munch's famous painting *The Scream*. Mr Spanton, my art teacher, has never felt a big wow for this project. He says that I am a keen visual learner with a naturally artistic streak, but he also says that busying myself, week after week, with the mere duplication of an expressionist painting depicting existential angst is both creatively limiting and likely to induce panic attacks. These were his EXACT words and I've learned them off by heart because they sound amazingly clever. Mr Spanton was laughing when he said this to me so I laughed back a bit – but I can't, one hundred per cent, hand on heart, honestly say that I totally understood what he was driving at. However he also said, 'And felt-tip pen doesn't look that good. You'd have been better off using chalk or oils.' This last bit I got. It's hard to take advice on board though when you've just wasted whole months of your life doing things wrong. So back then I'd just shrugged and picked up a chunky red felt-tip and carried on colouring in the sky.

But when I went to art today and saw that picture of the screaming skeleton with its hands over its ears and the world hemming it in like bars on a cage, I couldn't bear to get my felt-tips out. It reminded me of how I'd felt when I'd been sitting in my wardrobe thinking about all the reasons why I might want to jump out of my bedroom window and, frankly, that wasn't a very nice feeling to be reminded of. I suppose I finally understood what Mr Spanton was driving at. So I picked the whole 150 cm x 80 cm of it up and put it in the bin. And then I got out some oil paints and started a still-life portrait of a tomato-ketchup bottle. I feel much happier with this project.

2. The Sensitive Issue of Gareth Stingecombe Who Is Nice

It occurred to me today in art, while I was sketching the outline of a tomato-ketchup bottle, that I have not always been that nice to Gareth Stingecombe. I've never been deliberately horrible to him either, but I haven't actually always been terribly nice. Certainly not as nice as he deserves. I don't know why I haven't been nice because Gareth Stingecombe is a nice person. Actually he is very nice. He is so nice that he was prepared to rip the head off Lee Fogel and get himself excluded forever in defence of my honour. I don't actually approve of violence, but that was still nice of him. A few weeks ago he also asked me to the school disco. Twice. This was nice of him as well. I, however, was not nice. If I remember rightly, I said no to him the first time and laughed in his face the second. I didn't mean to laugh in his face, and I certainly didn't mean anything nasty by it but the fact does remain that Gareth Stingecombe asked me to the school disco and I laughed in his face. And that is not nice. And now I regret doing that. Gareth Stingecombe has also got a nice face and a nice smile and colossal manly thighs. Very recently, for some totally weird reason, I've been having random thoughts about those colossal manly thighs. When I have these thoughts, my face goes hot. I had one of these thoughts while I was drawing my tomato-ketchup bottle in art this morning and the shape of the bottle went all wonky. This is all very weird because in NO WAY would I previously EVER have said that I had sexual designs on Gareth Stingecombe, but now, actually, I think that it is time to confront the issue head on and deal with the truth.

I fancy Gareth Stingecombe.

At break-time I asked Goose what she thought about the hot flushes I've been getting as a result of random thoughts about Gareth's thighs. Goose said, 'I reckon it means you badly crave his body.'

When she said this I laughed really loudly and said, 'Don't be daft, Goose. This is Gareth Stingecombe we're talking about. He's got size sixteen feet and can't dance.'

Goose, who is a bit more experienced in matters of the heart than I am, said, 'Yeah, but, Lotts, how would you feel if you saw Gareth Stingecombe with his tongue jammed down someone else's throat?'

And when she said this I was speechless for quite a while because I understood, right then and there, that I wouldn't like it at all. Not one bit. And not in the put-out, left-out, on-the-shelf, no-mates, feeling-a-gooseberry, potty-Lottie kind of way that I'd felt when Goose went out with Neil Adam. Not like that. If I saw Gareth Stingecombe kissing someone else, it would just make me feel really very sad.

Because *I* want to kiss him.

When I didn't answer Goose's question she did a big dramatic sigh and said, 'I suppose it's just as well I took the chance of buying you a ticket for the school disco before they all sold out. Something tells me you'd quite like to go now. Am I right or am I right?'

And then she grinned and gave me a big hug right in the middle of the Year 10 yard. Goose is the best friend I could ever have. She is awesome.

3. The Sensitive Issue of my Former Status as a Thief

And this is the most sensitive issue of all. I can just about tolerate being called a schizo and I can also just about tolerate finding *Lottie Biggs is Mad* written on the door of a toilet cubicle because, inside, I know that neither of these labels, however true or untrue, is anything to be ashamed of. In fact, all that these labels reveal is that whoever uses them has a brain the size of a particularly small amoeba. Like this.

[22]

But what I can't tolerate is the idea that ANYONE might stop to consider me for a moment and then think, 'Oh yeah, Lottie Biggs, she's a thief.'

This is not the impression I want to make on people. Not even people like Gina.

So I have tackled the issue head on and dealt with it.

When I got home from school today, my mum was waiting in the kitchen to see how everything had gone. I told her I'd had an OK day and that she absolutely, definitely MUST go back to work tomorrow because my head feels fairly normal. She was very pleased when I said this and gave me a big hug. I'm getting an awful lot of hugs at the moment, which is quite weird to be honest because I'm not sure that I totally

---

[22] Or in other words, a brain which can only be seen with the aid of a super-strength microscope.

deserve them. And then I asked her what she'd done with all that swag I'd kept hidden in my wardrobe.

My mum looked a bit worried and said, 'Why? What do you want it for?'

'I'm gonna take it all back,' I said.

My mum cupped her chin in her hand and looked at me. Behind her, the kettle boiled and she made us both a cup of coffee and then we sat down at the kitchen table. After a bit she said, 'Well, I think that's a very good intention, Lottie. To be honest, I've been absolutely unable to decide what to do with it myself. It's all in bags in my bedroom and it worries me every time I look at it. But I'm not sure that taking it all back is the best thing for you to do right at this moment. You're just recovering from a colossal mood swing and I don't want you to get stressed out again. The people in those shops might not understand.'

I said, 'You're a Detective Sergeant. I don't think it's beneficial to your career to be harbouring stolen goods in your house.'

My mum sighed. 'No, it probably isn't.'

'And anyway,' I said, 'I'm OK. I feel a lot more positive about everything now that I know I'm a bit mental. So those chats with Dr Edwards have helped a lot and I even feel OK about having to have those stupid counselling sessions. Does that make sense?'

My mum thought about this for a moment and then she sort of nodded her head. She looked a bit worried. I don't know why though. I was feeling positive.

'I'll be OK, honest. I'll do it without getting in trouble. And I'll just start with Whitchurch today. Please, Mum – I really need to.'

My mum looked up at the ceiling a moment as if she was saying a prayer and then she said, 'Do you want me to come with you?'

'No.' I wasn't lying. Would *you* want your mum with you while you were on a shoplifting clean-up mission?

'OK. Do what you need to do. But phone me if you have any trouble and COME STRAIGHT HOME.'

Five minutes later I left the house. I had two bags with me. The larger one was a black plastic bin bag full of Sole Mates swag. The shoes made it very awkward to carry. The second, smaller, bag contained a plug-in air freshener, a toy giraffe and a pack of fifty clothes pegs. It was this smaller bag that I planned to get rid of first.

When I got to Pound World it was already four o'clock and the shop was nearly empty. I went straight to the counter. I put the smaller bag down in front of the girl sitting at the checkout and said, 'I got these things from here but now I don't want them.'

The girl looked a bit surprised and said, 'We don't do refunds.'

'That's OK,' I said. 'I don't want one.'

And then I walked out really quickly.

After that, I went up the road to Sole Mates. I knew this would be harder but there was no way I was bottling out. I just did my best not to think about it and concentrated as hard as I could on being positive. It was quite tricky, to be honest.

I walked into Sole Mates and put my black bin bag down on the floor. Dionne was standing by the till and sticking some YOU PAY stickers into some sandals I had never seen before and didn't know the name of. When she saw me, she looked up and said, 'Hello, Lottie. This is a surprise.'

It was a surprise for me too. I don't think I've ever once seen Dionne on the shop floor.

I said, 'I've brought all this stuff back.' And then I said, 'Where's Gina?'

Dionne smiled. 'She's left.'

I was so surprised by this that I forgot about being positive and went a bit blank. But only for a moment.

'Left? Where's she gone?'

Dionne smiled again and pointed towards the shop window and straight across the road. 'She's gone to work for Keith Bright. They're madly in love. A couple of weeks ago Keith finally plucked up the courage to come over and ask Gina out, and they've been inseparable ever since. And now she's working for him.'

My mouth fell open. 'Good God!' I said. 'Gina and Keith Bright – good God!'

'Everyone has their perfect person out there waiting for them. He's had his eye on her for ages,' said Dionne.

I looked out of the window and across the road. Keith Bright was no longer staring straight at Sole Mates, hoping desperately for a glimpse of me and Goose. I realized then that he never had been.

I stood there feeling supremely stupid and then I quietly said, 'When you next see Gina, will you please tell her that I'm not really a thief and I'm sorry, I really am.'

Dionne nodded. I turned to leave, but before passing through the door I paused and said, 'Oh, and Dionne, thanks for coming to my house the other day and telling me about your friend. I'm sorry I sat in my wardrobe the whole time.'

And then I felt a bit flustered and left.

the truth aBOut eLvis PresLeY

Elvis Presley is a fat man in his fifties who wears a very scruffy black leather jacket and spends most of his time asleep on a bench in the public garden in the centre of Whitchurch. When he's not asleep he sings Elvis Presley songs into a plastic toy microphone. He's got quite a good voice, but he doesn't really sound like the genuine Elvis because the genuine Elvis has an American accent, whereas this Elvis Presley is definitely from up the valleys.

Elvis Presley has been a regular feature of the public garden for as long as I can remember. So have an ever-changing crowd of sixth-form goths, but most of these are fairly ugly, to be honest. Every day I pass the public garden on my way to school, and every day I hear people from my school call Elvis Presley names. I have heard them call him a tramp, a bum, an alky, a homeless, a saddo, a wino, a junkie, a crusty, a madman, a bin-man, a nut-nut, a soap-dodger, a pikey and a schizo. I have heard them call Elvis all of these things. I myself have never called Elvis names because I reckon it's a better policy to smile at people. However, I am ashamed to admit that I may have *thought* he was some of these things, but I still definitely never called him any of them.

On my way back home after the shoplifting clean-up mission I passed by the public garden and Elvis Presley was sitting on the bench. As I walked by he called out, 'Hello, shoe-shop girl.'

I slowed down a bit and said, 'I don't work there any more. I got the sack.'

Elvis Presley shook his head and said, 'That's bad news, young lady. You don't want to make a habit of that.'

I said, 'Since when have you been a careers advisor?'

Elvis Presley laughed and said, 'I haven't never, have I? I'm a singer. I'm an entertainer. My job is to bring happiness and joy to the people of Whitchurch. And I do it like this.' And then he picked up his toy mike and started singing 'Hound Dog' to me and whoever else might be passing. But mostly he sang it to himself.

And I walked on then and I was smiling. Elvis Presley had made me smile with his cheery laugh and his toy microphone and his funny Welsh-Elvis singing voice. And he might just be a fat man in his fifties who wears a scruffy black leather jacket and drinks far too much and has no money and sleeps on a bench, and he may well be a little bit mad too, but I reckon it still takes a very special talent to be able to make other people smile. It takes no talent at all to make them feel awful. The kids who walk past Elvis Presley and call him names should remember that.

a Brief wOrD aBOut the eNDiNG

Dear Mr (or Mrs) Examiner

It's now nine o'clock on the evening of Tuesday 15 July and my personal writing project for GCSE English coursework is due in tomorrow. I've spent a lot of hours writing it. A LOT OF HOURS. In fact, I wouldn't be at all surprised if I've spent more time on this project than any other member of my English class. And I've really enjoyed writing it – except when I've been totally miserable – and I've got really heavily into it. But now it's nearly finished I have a problem. I don't know how to end it. When I saw Mr Wood today he suggested I end it with a sentence that begins in one of the following ways:

And that was when I discovered . . .

The most important thing I learned from this incident was . . .

This experience changed me because . . .

These suggestions are all very well and good but, as I explained to him, I haven't focused on one specific incident; I've kind of just written about my life as it's been happening.

When I told Mr Wood this, he nodded his head thoughtfully and said, 'The wider approach is OK, Charlotte, but specifics are good for detail, and detail is good for creative writing. I hope you've managed to put enough interesting detail in there.'

I said, 'I reckon so. I've written about fifty thousand words.'

When I said that, Mr Wood went very still and very white. For a moment I thought he might actually be having a funny turn. And then he said, 'Wow! That'll take some reading. I hope it's good.'

I said, 'I think so. I mean, I hope so.'

Mr Wood scratched his head and said, 'Have you read it all through and checked it for mistakes?'

I said, 'I don't need to read it through. I already know what it says.'

Mr Wood bit his lip and smiled at the same time and said, 'Hmm.' And then he said, 'What's it called?'

I was a bit confused when he asked me this because it seemed like a blatantly stupid question.

'It's called Extended Personal Writing,' I said.

Mr Wood shook his head. 'No, no, no, Charlotte. If you've spent nearly an entire term writing something which is fifty thousand words long, it deserves a proper title, don't you think?'

And then I saw what he was getting at and, yes, I *did* think it deserved a proper title.

But the thing is, I can't think of a good title and I can't think of a good ending so I'll just have to wait until tomorrow and hope that something comes to me then.

the Last Bit

My name is Lottie Biggs and a few weeks ago I was fifteen years old. At school, some people like to write *Lottie Biggs is Mad* on the doors of the cubicles in the girls' toilets. I don't find this particularly funny but I'm not going to let it wind me up because, right now, I am learning to deal with much heavier stuff that is happening in my life. I am five foot and half an inch tall and my hair colour is recently applied Melody Classic Ash with Foxy Red lowlights. My eyes are blue, my chin has a dimple in it and my nose is not classically pretty but definitely an interesting shape. My favourite subjects are English, history and art, and I am currently sitting in the school library typing up the VERY LAST BIT of my personal writing project for English coursework. So far I have written just under fifty thousand words. This morning, when I showed Mr Wood how much I'd written, he said, 'Well, Charlotte, you are definitely something special!' And then he gave me a commendation for exceptional effort. I asked Mr Wood if I could hand my project in after lunch as I wanted to use the lunch hour to write an interesting ending and that is what I am doing right now.

Before I went to English this morning I had two problems. The first problem was that I couldn't think of a good title for this project, but then I nipped to the loo during break and the answer suddenly became obvious. I won't bother telling you what title I chose because you've already seen it on the front of my work.

The second problem was that I had absolutely no idea how I was ever going to end this piece of coursework but now I do. And it's thanks partly to that poet woman, Stevie Smith. Today with Mr Wood we were looking at a poem right near the very back of the book. It was a poem about a man who has been messing about in the sea and suddenly realizes that he has got out of his depth. He tries to alert the attention of the people on the beach but because he's a silly, fun character, everyone just thinks he's waving at them and playing around. Nobody realizes he is in serious trouble until it's too late. The poem is called 'Not Waving but Drowning.'

When Mr Wood read this to us, I had an out-of-body experience. My mind floated right up to the ceiling of the classroom and, for a moment, it felt like I was looking down on myself from way up high. Except that the Lottie I saw was sitting in her wardrobe. And then I saw my ex-manageress, Dionne. She was looking a bit upset and telling me about her friend who'd had a problem with her head and got into loads of trouble in order to get the attention and help she desperately needed. Inside my wardrobe I was pretty close to crying because I understood it all too well. And then my mind tuned back into the lesson and I realized with the biggest WOW that me and Stevie Smith are not so very, very different. Stevie might be a famous English poet with a man's name and I might be a fifteen-year-old Welsh schoolgirl from Whitchurch in Cardiff with a funny nose, but me and Stevie both know what it's like to find yourself suddenly out of your depth. And as I sat there at my desk I felt a sense of real gratitude that Stevie Smith had written a poem about it. It was like she'd written that poem especially for me and I will remember that poem forever. And unlike the unlucky man in that poem, I'm not going to drown because the people around me will always be watching to see if I wave.

But I said it's thanks *partly* to Stevie Smith. The other person I need to thank for helping me with this ending is a certain boy who has a nice face, very big feet and colossal rugby thighs. At break-time I was sitting in the yard eating pizza with Goose when I saw Gareth Stingecombe leaning against the wall of the gym and fiddling with his iPod. I said to Goose, 'Wait here a second,' and I walked over and tapped him on the arm.

'All right, Biggsy?' he said, flicking one of his earphones out of his ear.

'Gareth,' I said, 'I was wondering – you know the end of term disco on Friday? I was wondering if you're still going.'

Gareth Stingecombe stopped fiddling with his iPod and gave me a half-playful, half-suspicious look. 'Might be. Why?'

I shrugged my shoulders and said, 'Well, if you *are* going, and you're not going with anyone in particular if you know what I mean, well, it would be really good to see you there.'

I could feel my cheeks burning but, hey, I'd said it.

Gareth smiled. 'Really good or *really* good?'

I bit my lip to stop myself from smiling too much. '*Really* good,' I said.

Gareth smiled even more and said, 'You know what? It would be *really* good to see you there too.' And then he gave me a big beaming grin and punched me in the arm. Not hard. Just friendly.

And that was when I discovered that I *really, really* like being me.

Hayley Long would like to say a big

thank you to

Ruth and everyone at Macmillan,
all the nice people at Pollinger – especially Yeelesy,
Gwen Davies and Annes for reading Biggsy first,
Dr Anne Bryan and Professor John Lazarus for being
handy medical experts,
Milesy from the Cardiff Boys and Girls in Blue for showing
me inside a cell and then letting me out again,
Bethan Batten for giving me some Welsh words,
Graham Tomlinson for being all-round generally fab

and everyone at Paston College, Norfolk
for being so totally lush

and finally to Whitchurch High School,
Cardiff, for giving me loads of inspiration.

Diolch yn fawr [23]

---

[23] Which means **Thank you very much** in Welsh.

aBOut the authOr

haYLeY LONG was born in Ipswich ages ago. She studied English at university in Wales, where she had a very nice time and didn't do much work. After that she spent several years in various places abroad and had a very nice time and didn't do much work then either. Now **haYLeY** is an English **teaCher** and works very hard indeed. She lives in Norwich with a **raBBit** called **irma** and a **husBaND**. *Lottie Biggs Is (Not) Mad* is her first novel for young adults – but there will be more from **LOttie** (and **haYLeY**) **COmiNG sOON.**

if YOu ever fiND YOurseLf sittiNG iN a warDrOBe
wONDeriNG what Life is aLL aBOut, there are LOts
Of weBsites aND PeOPLe YOu CaN CaLL tO fiND
Out mOre aBOut hOw YOu are feeL NG:

www.**teeNissues**.co.uk

www.**saNe**.OrG.uk
☎ **08457 67 80 00**

www.**ChaNNeL4**.cOm/heaLth/miCrOsites/0-9/4heaLth/teeNLife/

samarItaNs – PrOviDiNG 24-hOur
CONfiDeNtiaL emOtiONaL suPPOrt fOr PeOPLe iN NeeD
☎ **08457 90 90 90**

suPPOrtLiNe – PrOviDiNG CONfiDeNtiaL
emOtiONaL suPPOrt iN Part CuLar fOr ChiLDreN aND YOuNG aDuLts
ON a varietY Of issues iNCLuDiNG stress, DePressiON aND aNXietY
☎ **020 8554 9004**

Or YOu CaN aLwaYs taLk tO sOmeONe
CLOse tO YOu:
YOur famiLY, a frieND, a DOCtOr, a teaCher –
it wOrkeD fOr LOttie N **the eND!**

Lottie Biggs is NOT Desperate

Hayley Long

whY am I eDGY as aN eGGsheLL? am I **DOOmeD** tO Be a traGIC DesPeraDO mY whOLe Life? am I stILL **maD**? If NOt, whY am I seeING a GuIDaNCe COuNseLLOr (whO LOOks LIke JOhNNY DePP)? aND whY am I BeING kePt awake BY a **hYPeraCtIve GerIatrIC ChINChILLa** aND INDeCeNt vIsIONs Of Gareth stINGeCOmBe wearING hIs DaD's **BrItNeY sPears BOXer shOrts**? wILL I ever stOP BeING a DesPerate tOtaL Utter vIrGIN?

YOu'LL have tO reaD mY New BOOk tO fIND Out!

COmING sOON . . .

A selected list of titles available from Macmillan Children's Books

The prices shown below are correct at the time of going to press. However, Macmillan Publishers reserves the right to show new retail prices on covers, which may differ from those previously advertised.

Julia Bell		
Dirty Work	978-0-330-44571-9	£5.99
Julie Burchill		
Sugar Rush	978-0-330-41583-5	£5.99
Meg Cabot		
Airhead	978-0-330-45382-0	£9.99
Jaclyn Moriarty		
Finding Cassie Crazy	978-0-330-41803-4	£5.99

All Pan Macmillan titles can be ordered from our website, www.panmacmillan.com, or from your local bookshop and are also available by post from:

Bookpost, PO Box 29, Douglas, Isle of Man IM99 1BQ

Credit cards accepted. For details:
Telephone: 01624 677237
Fax: 01624 670923
Email: bookshop@enterprise.net
www.bookpost.co.uk

Free postage and packing in the United Kingdom